Micheline's hand rested on the arm of a handsome, well-muscled man…

He turned at something Micheline said, and a devastating smile split his black face. He was the man she had seen on the plane! Sweat trickled under Lorraine's arms. Someone had lit a fire inside her!

"Lorraine," her friend said in French, "I would like you to meet His Excellency Monsieur Momar Diallo."

The man from the airplane held out a long, slender black hand toward her. But Lorraine's brain had gone lame Lorraine was more firmly bewitched than she had ever been in her life His presence was overpowering…

He leaned toward her, and she could feel him trembling throughout his body. Her own body trembled, too, and she felt like a drum somebody had hit very hard. She turned her willing mouth to him and he took it, easily. His warm, soft lips touched hers in a sweetly seductive kiss.

WHISPERS IN THE SAND

LAFLORYA GAUTHIER

Genesis Press, Inc.

Indigo Love Stories

An imprint of Genesis Press, Inc.
Publishing Company

Genesis Press, Inc.
P.O. Box 101
Columbus, MS 39703

ISBN-13: 978-1-58571-304-2
ISBN-10: 1-58571-304-x
Manufactured in the United States of America

First Edition 1996
Second Edition 2008

Visit us at www.genesis-press.com or call at 1-888-Indigo-1

DEDICATION

This book is dedicated to my late husband whom I thank for his patience and love. Thanks for technical help goes to: E. Vincent Holten and Maurice Quinn for the information about filming. Ousseynou Diop for his information about circumcision initiations in the Ziguinchor area.

1

Momar Diallo was fuming. He could no longer hold back his resentment. Snarling under his breath, he spoke out. "Damn it, I'm a diplomat, not a diplomatic courier or a diplomatic escort!"

The chauffeur turned around in the front seat of the air-conditioned luxury car. "What, sir?"

"Nothing," Momar snapped, fearing he would explode with anger. The handsome young man turned and glared angrily at the entrance to the Senegalese Embassy. He wondered how much longer he would have to wait. No one in Dakar had told him that at the end of June, Washington, D. C. would be hotter than the capital of Sénégal! He had almost fainted upon arrival the day before when the hot, humid air had struck his face as he stepped outside the airport in Washington. But now his anger was rising to match the soaring temperature. He resented the degradation of this assignment, not to mention the overwhelming arrogance of the foreign minister.

Here he was, having been an ambassador plenipotentiary, with an unblemished service record to more than five countries, sitting in the back seat of an embassy car, waiting to escort a disgraced diplomat home. As the foreign minister had explained, Momar had been given the assignment because he was between postings, he spoke English fluently, and he could be trusted with a confidential assignment. In addition, he'd been the one selected to take an emergency diplomatic pouch to Washington.

Some obscure, perverse instinct in Momar made him suspect that it was because he was a griot by birth. The foreign minister was from a so-called superior tribe, and Momar wondered if the man felt that a griot, no matter what his personal accomplishments, would have to obey even when the assignment was beneath him. Momar fumed anew at the memory of the interview. In his current mood of outrage, he was ready to come to any conclusion, look for devious motives in anything.

Now, he was waiting impatiently for Ambassador Lo to personally escort the failed diplomat to his embassy car. The culprit was the reason the Foreign Minister had shown Momar the emergency diplomatic pouch delivery.

Momar knew that Omar Sall had been summarily dismissed from his Senegalese diplomatic post for dishonoring it. Sall had been heavily investing money that did not belong to him, and he'd participated in a private American firm of questionable reputation. Sall's diplomatic covering had not made him immune to weakness, greed, stupidity and bad companions.

"And to think that he was offered that post when everyone knew I was ahead of him for it," Momar murmured, this time too low for the chauffeur to hear him.

The embassy's front door opened, and Momar Diallo sought to control the rage in his mind and heart as he hopped quickly from the big car. He stood beside the chauffeur as the ambassador escorted the disgraced Omar Sall to the car. They were followed by an embassy flunky, who carried the one suitcase Sall was allowed to take with him.

Momar bowed slightly, acknowledging the ambassador's somewhat embarrassed greeting.

"Mr. Diallo, you know that you are not to leave Mr. Sall's side until you are met in Dakar," said the ambassador, a very tall, jet black, serious Ouloff.

"Yes, sir. I remember my instructions, Mr. Ambassador," he said, standing aside for Sall, an obese man of middle age, who was clad in a white djellaba, white babouches and no hat. Entering the back seat, Sall seemed more shaken than the day before when Momar had first seen him. Sall's black eyes had the look of a whipped dog as he sat on the far side of the seat, sighing heavily and clasping his hands tightly together.

Having finished giving his instructions, the ambassador turned and reentered the building while the flunky and the chauffeur arranged Sall's suitcase in the front seat of the car.

Momar gladly returned to the car. The heat of the sidewalk had begun to burn his feet through the thin soles of his summer babouches.

He had instructions to board the Air Afrique flight to Dakar at the last possible minute in order to attract as little attention as possible. The ambassador was well aware of Sénégal's Radio Tam Tam, and he was concerned that any bad news about a diplomat might adversely affect his own position.

There was maybe one good thing that could come from this hateful mission, Momar told himself. The ambassador had taken him into his confidence; thus, the man might put in a good word for him at the Foreign Ministry back in Dakar. Momar dearly wanted to be posted to the embassy in Washington. Who would not? It was next to being posted to the United Nations in New York or to the embassy in Paris, France. He certainly had the seniority and the necessary qualifications, he mused, though it was a long way from his humble origins. As the powerful car sped them toward Washington's Dulles Airport, Momar sat back and recounted his past.

Even though he had finished at the lycée with the highest marks in its history, there was little hope for him to continue his education at that time. His family was from that section of the Ouloff tribe known as griots. Griots are primarily oral historians, but they also work as artisans. Historically their duties had been to maintain the verbal history of the ruling tribes. They also made the harnesses that the ruling warriors used on their proud Arabian horses. They made the sandals that the warriors wore. They made the scabbards for the warriors' swords and embroidered the finery for the warriors' battle clothing.

Momar was the first of his family to finish at the lycée without knowing how to play the kora or how to recount the history of his traditional tribal masters back to twenty generations and more at weddings, baptisms and funerals. His family and his circumcision companions considered him an aberration.

The French, who ran the lycée in those days, also considered him a rare bird indeed. Like most Ouloffs, he was tall and thin; but he was always so intense. Most of the time his head was in a book. When school closed, the year he graduated, he left Dakar for Casamance to ask his father for guidance about his future. The day after his arrival, the quiet tranquility of their tiny village was turned upside down. A postman from Dakar came looking for him, and all of the villagers were certain that he had committed some terrible crime at the lycée. But they were as dumbfounded as Momar and his family when the postman announced that Momar was to accompany him back to Dakar. He had with him a ticket to Paris! He had been accepted to the Sorbonne!

That night the village threw him a going-away party, during which his family recounted their own history and Momar's accomplishments.

The following morning, Momar set out at dawn in the rattle-trap jalopy with the postman.

Until this day, he could not remember a single part of that trip or the plane ride to Paris. It was like a fantastic dream that fades fast upon awakening.

During his years at the university, he could not visit home, even during the summer holidays, because there was not enough money.

After obtaining his master's degree in International Relations, the only place he could think of to apply, upon returning home, was the Ministry of Foreign Affairs. Because he had learned English very well, thanks to an English girlfriend during those years, Momar's first posting was at the Senegalese embassy in Monrovia, Liberia. That had been ten years ago.

Since then, he had been posted all over Africa, sometimes in English-speaking countries, sometimes in French-speaking ones.

His most recent posting had been to Zaire. That posting had ended when his Zairian wife had been killed in a car accident. He had asked for, and had been granted, an immediate leave of absence.

While Momar had long dreamed of a posting to Washington or Paris, he still was not certain that he was psychologically ready. Perhaps, he conceded, the foreign minister just might have sent him on this mission to test him. But his mission was so brief that he had seen little of the famous American capital and nothing of New York. What a disappointing waste of his time, he thought as they pulled into Dulles Airport for their shuttle flight to New York.

When Lorraine Barbette boarded the flight to Dakar, she was still smarting from last week's run-in with her now ex-fiancé back in their home town of Mound Bayou, Mississippi. Tired and disturbed, she had not even protested when the purser had explained that they had overbooked. Apologizing profusely, he'd told them that one of her party of three would have to sit in first class.

Her two colleagues had taken one look at her sad, tired face and nominated her for the honor. She'd nodded distractedly and flopped down. She didn't even react when they teased her about sneaking free champagne back to their crowded section of the plane. Lorraine had simply fastened her seat belt and stared out of the plane's small window. She hadn't even bothered to look around when, seconds before the doors closed for takeoff, two men hastened aboard and took the seats across the aisle from hers.

Not until their flight attendant served champagne and offered her a choice of perfume did Lorraine venture a glance at the last-minute arrivals. Dove-gray eyes collided with jet black ones. The younger man was staring at her with the boldest, yet friendliest and most disturbingly deep black eyes she'd ever seen. The look made her throat constrict. Never in her life had she seen eyes so hypnotic. They glinted with crystal reflections. His black face seemed to be carved in ebony planes. It contained an ancient handsomeness that carried the history of his people.

Her glance turned into a stare. His hair had the velvety darkness of a night without moonlight. There was not even a glint in it. Then, his companion, a middle-aged man dressed in a white Senegalese djellaba, said something in a language that Lorraine did not know and the younger man turned toward his seat companion.

Lorraine felt both bewitched and confused. This man's deep ebony eyes disturbed her far more than her ex-fiancé's familiar brown ones ever had.

Momar Diallo fastened his seat belt, stretched his long legs to their full length and tried to study his fellow passengers. His eyes always returned, as if of their own volition, to the young, elegantly dressed, tan-skinned woman across the aisle from him. He heard nothing of the takeoff instructions, nor could he remember what Sall had said to him a moment ago, which seemed to anger the older man. Snapping his seat belt around his ample middle, Sall simply stared angrily out the window.

Focusing again on the young woman, Momar decided the girl was a beauty, even if skinny by his standards. Her nose was thin, and her mouth was soft, shapely, if a little sad looking. Her skin color seemed to him like that of honey made from goldenrods. Her hair was thick, jet black, and she wore it long.

He watched boldly as she put up a well-manicured hand and stroked an errant strand. He wondered what it would feel like to stroke her mane. Long and silky, it would feel sexy, he was sure. She glanced around again, and their gaze locked once more. Her dove gray eyes were long lashed. He sighed.

Momar unsnapped his seat belt and shifted his weight as he accepted the after-shave lotion gift and a soft drink from their cabin attendant.

Why was he so captivated by this girl? He had not been interested in a woman since...he could not remember. He had not been in love with his wife. Theirs had been an arranged marriage. Yes, it had been a very long time. Too long, he decided. This woman probably would not give him the time of day. She had the look of one of those rich African-American women who sometimes traveled to Africa in search of their roots, inspired, no doubt, by the book of the same name.

Lorraine was bone tired. She closed her eyes and tried not to think; but her mind insisted on replaying that last evening with Andrew in Mound Bayou, a place that had never felt right for her. It was a beautiful, mellow summer night. But Lorraine was sad. She and Andrew should have been on friendlier terms. But ever since she had come home on this visit, he had been touchy and overly sensitive to her remarks. She wondered why he couldn't understand her point of view. Instead, here they were tense and upset, arguing again.

Andrew had done his university and post-graduate work at Ole Miss. Thanks to the civil rights movement, African-Americans were a common sight on the campus these days. He'd returned to Mound Bayou to become the high school principal. For now he was content, but one day he planned to become mayor. Maybe more, with both Lorraine's family and his own behind him. Lorraine knew she was a valuable acquisition. But though Andrew had a disciplined, organized life, he could be petulant, quick-tempered and surly.

She could hardly believe it was only last week when they were strolling along and Andrew said that she'd been chosen for this assignment only because of her color. That hurt.

Shocked, Lorraine stopped and cried, glaring into Andrew's face. "What a rotten thing to say. Can't you accept that I'm the producer and director on this assignment?"

Hoping to diffuse his hostility, she reminded him, "I'd like to think that the years I spent both in universities learning French and in my profession are part of it, Andrew. You seem to forget that I've worked for five long years with this company."

"Okay. I agree to that, but I still can't see why you won't set a date for our wedding," Andrew countered stubbornly, this time without the hostility in his voice.

It irked her to think he had such little regard for her ambitions. She resumed walking, Andrew beside her.

She spoke firmly into the ensuing silence, still somewhat peeved. "Andrew, you and I have known each other all our lives. Our families have arranged this marriage. But you seem to want something very different than I do." She stopped, hands on hips, facing him. When he didn't reply, she continued, "You want to be elected mayor. You and I know that unless you marry the big-shot preacher's daughter that won't be possible. I should never have allowed such an arrangement to get this far in the first place."

Andrew was silent.

"Don't you see, Andrew?" she cried. "I need my own career."

"That's your problem," Andrew finally said in a harsh voice.

Lorraine was still attempting to make him understand. "Don't you remember when we were children how I always dreamed of working in films? So now I've got the chance to do something really exciting. And you don't even care. All you care about is your own ambition!" She had shouted the last sentence. Somewhat sarcastically, she cried, "Marry. Become Mrs. Big Shot Andrew Kemp, the principal's wife, later the mayor's wife and then what, Andrew?"

It was too dark to see his reaction, so when he still didn't speak, Lorraine continued, unable to stem her frustration.

"To be frank with you, I was going to call off our engagement anyway. I don't think it's fair to either of us to marry simply to please our families."

She went on as though talking to herself. "Andrew, when I won that scholarship to Concordia University in Montreal and then another to do my graduate work at the University of Montreal, I was in seventh heaven."

"And don't you see, Lorraine, I was in seventh hell," Andrew retorted, his voice on edge again.

"But we saw each other the summers I came home," said Lorraine. "We kept in touch. And you always knew my ambitions. Besides, I never promised I would quit my career and move back to Mound Bayou. I never lied to you. Ever."

She could tell by the stubborn set of his shoulders that Andrew only understood what he wanted to understand. She had tried to prevent an argument with him on this trip, but she realized finally that the engagement was a sham, and Andrew was ready to go through with the sham marriage to further his own ambitions. He couldn't understand why Lorraine would not live a sham life.

Arguing with him, she decided at last, was like trying to unscramble an egg. With an exasperation she tried to mask, she clamped her well-shaped lips and resignedly stared off into the rural darkness...

"Good morning, ladies and gentlemen..."

Lorraine woke with a start, her right arm slightly numb. She realized suddenly that she was not back home in Mound Bayou but flying high above the Atlantic Ocean. She rubbed her eyes and smoothed her dress over slim legs, which were stretched in front of her seat. Someone had covered her with a blanket during the night. She shook it off and folded it onto the empty seat beside her.

"This is the captain speaking. Breakfast will be served in a few minutes. We are on schedule for our arrival at Dakar-Yoff Airport." A short time later, they were on the ground. The entire plane had to wait until the young Senegalese man and his older companion were whisked away, as if by magic, to an official-looking black car. Then the passengers and crew were allowed to disembark. Lorraine moved along with her group into the blazing early morning sunshine. "Whew! I wish the captain had mentioned the temperature," she said, wiping her brow with a tissue. Her two male companions had removed their jackets and rolled up the sleeves of their shirts. They were both perspiring profusely. Walking was like wading into an oven.

Ebony porters, airline workers and customs agents swarmed about in a haze of brilliant local costumes.

Lorraine joined the other passengers and her two colleagues Sam Benson, their scheduling boss, and Mark Whitman, their cameraman. They waited at the luggage table in front of the customs agent.

"*Bonjour, mademoiselle. Avez-vous quelque chose a declarer?*" (Have you anything to declare?) asked a young, jet black customs agent. He wore a wrinkled khaki safari suit. He eyed her curiously, his marking crayon poised expectantly above her expensive, red leather suitcase.

"*Bonjour, monsieur. Non. Je n'ai rien a declarer.*" (I have nothing to declare.) Lorraine grinned for the first time since she had left New York. She wiped her olive-colored face with a new tissue and looked around for someplace to discard the other one. The heat was terrible.

The customs agent grinned in response, marked her suitcase, and allowed her to join to Sam and Mark. *Got through that all right,* she thought with a chuckle, *and I haven't used my French regularly since leaving Montreal five years ago!* She was startled when Sam gasped and exclaimed, "Why, Lorraine Barbette, you speak French like a native!"

"Well, not exactly like 'a native', Sam," she replied dryly, pulling her suitcase from the customs table, "but I do speak it well enough to get by."

Black porters and taxi drivers surged around them, grabbing at their suitcases as they left the customs area, quoting prices and arguing good-naturedly among themselves, confusing the newcomers.

After a few moments, however, a tall, jet black man in a white djellaba pushed his way toward them and yelled over the din in English, "Are you the Cultural Sights and Sounds film people?" All three of them nodded, fascinated by the scene unrolling around them.

Already Lorraine knew instinctively, in spite of Andrew's objections, that she had been right to insist on coming to Sénégal. She looked at the airport surroundings and felt, somehow, that this, now and here, was a turning point in her life. Her work meant a lot to her. She had a feeling about this assignment and about this place. Back home she had tried everything she knew to make Andrew understand how much her work meant to her.

"Now," she whispered, close to tears of pure joy, "my first overseas assignment." She felt like hugging herself, but instead she followed Sam and Mark into the minivan. They had been escorted to it by the tall black man who had introduced himself as Mansour Diop, explaining that he was to be their guide and chauffeur for the duration of their stay. They shook hands, and he had turned on the air conditioning before he began storing their baggage.

They arrived a few minutes later at the elegant white seaside Hotel N'Gor. Lorraine was swept along with everyone else to the reception desk, where they were assigned their rooms.

Lorraine Barbette was not normally a nervous person, but she was nervous and jittery now. She stroked her long hair. It was a habit she had when she was agitated.

Although she and Micheline Martin had kept in touch by letter, she had not talked with her friend for two years.

Micheline was First Secretary at the Canadian Embassy in Dakar, and they had been friends since their university days in Montreal. But seeing Micheline again was not the reason Lorraine was nervous.

How could she find the right words to ask her friend, whom she hadn't seen in years, about the disturbingly suave, handsome Senegalese man she had seen on the Air Afrique flight from New York?

Now here she was prowling her hotel room like a restless panther and trying to find the right words to use when she talked with her longtime friend.

Suddenly, Lorraine picked up the receiver and stabbed the telephone buttons before she lost courage. "Good morning. The Canadian Embassy," a pleasant voice answered in French.

Lorraine spoke rapidly in the same language. *"Mademoiselle Micheline Martin, s'il vous plaît.* I believe she is your First Secretary."

"One moment, please," the same melodious voice answered briskly. "Micheline Martin here. *Bonjour,"* a new female voice said after a moment.

"Micheline? It's Lorraine. Lorraine Barbette," the American woman replied, grinning widely for the second time since landing in Dakar. She was picturing her friend's reaction upon learning where she was telephoning from.

"Lorraine, what a clear line we have. You sound so close," Micheline gasped into her telephone.

"I'm in Dakar, at Hotel N'Gor!" Lorraine cried.

Micheline squealed in Lorraine's ear. "I cannot believe it! What are you doing here?"

Lorraine, relaxing by the second, gushed, "I work for this film company. But you already know that. Right?" Without giving her friend more than just enough time to give a sharp exhalation of breath, she rushed on, "Well, I'm here with colleagues to make a documentary film."

"When did you arrive?" Micheline asked breathlessly.

"We got in this morning on the Air Afrique flight from New York," Lorraine explained. "When can we get together? How long are you going to be here? Did Andrew come with you?"

"Hey, slow down. We'll be here for several weeks at least. Andrew isn't with me." Taking a deep breath, she added, "As a matter of fact, Andrew and I probably won't be seeing each other again any time soon."

There was a short, awkward pause before Micheline carefully replied, "I thought you two would have been married by now."

"When I was visiting Mound Bayou last week on holiday, I told him of my good fortune in getting this assignment, and we had a terrible fight, Micheline. He was dead set against my coming to Sénégal."

She closed her eyes, reliving the final scenes with Andrew.

"I see," her friend replied soberly. "One of those, eh?"

"Yes," Lorraine sighed.

"I am on my private line, Lorraine, and I am your friend. I sense there is something else you are not telling me, is there not? Will you tell me about it?"

The American woman sighed again. "Is it okay? You're sure?" She swallowed hard. She needed to talk to someone. She and Micheline had often shared their deepest secrets and feelings. Lorraine knew that Micheline was expecting her to talk more about her fight with Andrew, but she really wanted to talk about the mysterious stranger on the plane.

"I…I, oh, I don't know how to begin this Micheline. I flew over with no."

"What on earth are you trying to tell me, Lorraine?" Micheline was lost.

"Oh, I'm all flustered," Lorraine cried. "Well, I saw him on the plane, you see."

"No, I do not see, Lorraine. What are you trying to say? Saw who?" Her friend was totally confused now.

"That's exactly it! Who? There was this Senegalese man in the seat across the aisle from mine, and, and…."

"And what, Lorraine?"

"I'm behaving like a moonstruck school girl," Lorraine finished lamely, ashamed of herself.

"And?" Micheline prompted.

"Do you think you might know who he is?" Lorraine began and went on before her friend could utter a word. "I heard the cabin attendant call him *Monsieur* Diallo. And I saw M. D. engraved on his briefcase. He was traveling with a middle-aged man, and both of them left in an important-looking black limo," she finished, laughing a little as she remembered her unabashed spying.

Micheline let out a loud breath. "Lorraine Barbette, that is not at all like you! What has gotten into you? Have you the African fever already?" She began to laugh.

"Aha! You're laughing at me?" Lorraine was sorry she had been so silly. What a stupid sounding story.

But her friend was already answering her question. "Oh, that would be Momar Diallo."

Now it was Lorraine's turn to laugh and chide her friend. "Do you always know the Senegalese men traveling from New York so well?" She teased.

"No. Monsieur Diallo is a very important diplomat, and everyone knows he was sent to Washington to bring back one of their disgraced diplomats. Radio Tam Tam, you know."

"Radio Tam Tam? What's that, a local radio station?" she asked.

"Local gossip monger, my dear." It was Micheline's turn to laugh. "A local radio station, indeed!" She could not help laughing again.

"Oh." Lorraine felt disheartened. Why would 'a very important diplomat' even remember having seen her? She was a fool to have mentioned him. Micheline must think she'd lost her mind, she thought.

Micheline returned to the subject of Andrew, already dismissing the conversation about Diallo. "Tell me what happened between you and Andrew?" she prompted.

Hesitantly, Lorraine began, "You know he and I have been engaged to marry almost since our childhood. And, well, it was mostly because our two families are so close. They have always wanted the two families joined."

"And with you and Andrew they saw their chance?" Micheline interrupted angrily. "How archaic."

"I know, but that's often how it is with the so-called 'old line' families where I come from," Lorraine answered heavily.

Micheline paused for a moment. "Sounds like here," she said, then asked, "but how do you feel about such an arrangement?"

"To be quite frank with you, Micheline, when Andrew and I were adolescents I thought of him as a good and reliable friend. But I really can't say that he ever lit my fire, if you know what I mean." She chuckled. "Marrying him would be comfortable, predictable, stable…"

"And dull?" Micheline finished for her.

"You said it. But I always felt I had to marry him because our families took it for granted. His father and mine are co-pastors of our church. His mother and mine control the town's social and cultural life." How stupid it all sounded now, but she went on. "They expect him to be mayor one day, if we marry. Oh, it all sounds so cut and dried, doesn't it, Micheline?"

"Try and forget about all that now that you are in Sénégal. Try to enjoy your time here. Which reminds me, will you be coming to the reception at the Foreign Office tonight?" Micheline asked.

Lorraine brightened. "It's in our honor, my dear," she chirped. "Oh, Micheline. I'm so excited about that. It's certainly the first time I've ever been to a reception where I was one of the persons being honored. It sounds so, so…important!" She gushed.

"It is important," Micheline replied, laughing. "See you tonight then. And, Lorraine, I sincerely thank you for telephoning. It is simply great to hear from you again," she finished warmly.

"Same here," Lorraine replied, just as warmly. She felt much better now. They both rang off.

By the time their car had reached the Foreign Ministry building, Momar's anger and frustration had solidified to a hard lump in his chest. He watched as Sall was led away, where to, Momar did not know, nor did he care.

An hour later, just as he was congratulating himself on an unpleasant job well-done and was almost out the door, the foreign minister's secretary halted him. Momar knew he should have been suspicious when the minister, a short, thin Toucouleur, waved him into his office with a big smile. Momar had been caught off guard.

After both men were seated, the minister asked him about his trip, in detail. Then he gave him the highlights of the ambassador's written report and offered him tea.

Certain now that he was about to be named to a post in the United States, France or England, Momar relaxed and sipped his tea. Why else would the foreign minister himself get so cozy? Momar asked himself.

"Diallo," the minister said between loud sips of tea.

Here we go! he thought. *I have got my posting!*

"Er, Diallo," the minister was going on, "you handled this assignment so well that we have something else for you," he concluded expansively. *I do not like the sound of that 'something else,'* Momar thought. He tensed, waiting.

Without further preamble the minister let him have it: "There is a film crew just arrived in Dakar from America. They already have a guide and chauffeur, Mansour Diop, from the Ministry of Information, but I must assign a diplomatic escort from this office. And, since you speak English, you are our man! Ahem." The minister took another loud sip of his tea.

Momar almost spilled his. Another escort assignment! He almost screamed aloud.

Instead he choked out, "Ah, aah, *Monsieur le Ministre...*"

"I told the Minister of Information we could count on you, Diallo!" the minister said happily, reaching over the small, low table to vigorously shake Momar's hand.

"Your duties as the escort are limited. They will only need you weeks from now to smooth the waters in Ziguinchor. Their guide, Diop, will take care of them in the bigger cities," the foreign minister said, trying to appease Momar.

"By the time this assignment is over, I know for sure, an important post will be available for you. Go to the Ministry of Information tomorrow afternoon. They will give you more particulars." The minister finished in a dismissive tone. Momar knew the interview was over and there was no need to protest. But his mind viciously did: There is one available *now* in New York, and in Washington, and in Paris, and in London!

Momar wanted to cry. Not only was he an escort again, but he had been lent to another ministry! *Zut!* Damn! He fumed silently, all the while smiling weakly as the minister escorted him to the door. At least he was finally free to go home.

For the first time in a long time, however, home held no thrill for him. But he was tired and weary. Also, he could not forget the young woman he had seen on the plane.

"And, yes, damn it," he said to the sidewalk, "here I go escorting someone else. This time a whole crew of Americans! Allah save me." He stalked to where his car was parked, jerked open the door, and threw his carry-on bag and briefcase into the back seat. Both landed with a heavy thud. The briefcase tipped and fell to the floor. He never even noticed.

After angrily scrunching behind the steering wheel, Momar slammed the car door shut. He turned on the ignition and stomped on the gas to start his car. It jerked, as if it too was angry, then stopped dead. More carefully Momar eased the car from the parking lot and into traffic.

"I will bet those damned Americans are like that last bunch who went around trying to photograph the girls in

the countryside who went bare-chested," he spat, talking to
the car.

All they were interested in was looking for something
that would be sensational back in America. What a mess,
escorting an ignorant American film crew! "Momar, how
low can you get?" he asked himself.

When she put the telephone down, Lorraine headed for
the bathroom. The short talk with her friend had helped
her morale a lot.

"Wow! Am I in Africa or what?" She exclaimed, rele-
gating Andrew to the back of her mind. But she could not
do the same with the handsome diplomat she had seen on
the plane. She literally glided to the bathroom. Pale orange
and sand-colored hand-painted tiles covered the walls and
floor.

"I could swim in that tub," she cried, staring at the
biggest bathtub she had ever seen. One whole wall was a
mirror and she stared at herself and laughed out loud. She
was rumpled, her thick black hair was out of place, her
lipstick was smeared, but her dove gray eyes glowed with
delight as she turned the bathtub faucet to warm and added
perfumed oil to the water.

A few minutes later she sighed contentedly as she
lowered herself into the water richly perfumed with Chanel
19 bath oil. She was shocked to find that, reclining, her toes
did not touch the end of the tub even though she was tall
enough to be a fashion model. Nevertheless, she submerged
herself up to her neck, careful not to slide beneath the
water.

She sighed again. "This is Africa! This is Sénégal! And this is where that Monsieur Momar Diallo lives! Whoopee!" She felt like a school girl. She savored his name, recalling every detail of his face and his warm, brooding eyes. They had made her feel as though she had changed planets, not just countries and continents.

Much later, Lorraine turned on the bedside radio. The room was flooded immediately with an African song. She did not understand the words, but the song itself had a haunting quality to it. She recognized the dreamy sound of the kora, the guitar-like instrument she had once seen played when Les Ballets Africains had given a concert in New York. She listened a few minutes, her chin propped in her hands, then she turned the volume down, stretched luxuriously again, and was soon asleep.

2

The land that divided the highway leading from Hotel N'Gor to downtown Dakar was a rage of violent color. Flowers were blooming everywhere. The scenery that greeted them caused Lorraine's two colleagues to "ooh" and "aah" all the way into the city and across town to the Ministry of Foreign Affairs building on the edge of the Place de l'Indépendence.

Along the way Lorraine strained to see everything, from the prosperous looking two-story homes surrounded by high fences to the raw, tumbledown huts to the offices and government buildings on the Plateau, as the center of the city was called. The roads were crowded, jammed with cars, bicycles, carts, buses and gaily-painted mammy wagons, called car rapides in Sénégal. And there were groups of children who swarmed like flies.

Soon, their minivan passed the city hall and they arrived at their destination. Lorraine, Sam and Mark crowded into the reception hall of the Foreign Ministry.

Lorraine spotted Micheline immediately. She was standing beyond the reception line.

After Sam formally introduced Mark and Lorraine to the various dignitaries, Lorraine ran to her friend who was waving frantically. They embraced warmly and pecked each other on the cheeks, as they had done so often back in Montreal. Then, they stood back and admired each other, both grinning widely. Other arriving guests made a space around the happy pair of beautiful women.

"You have not changed at all," Micheline gushed in her strong French-Canadian accent, her cheerful blue eyes gazing admiringly at her American friend. Lorraine was wearing a strapless white silk dress which clung to her lithe body. Her open-toed black pumps completed her toilette. Her fondness for open-toed shoes, even during Montreal's winters, had been the joke among their friends back there.

"And you haven't changed either." Lorraine looked in wonder at her friend whose blonde hair had been bleached almost white by the African sun. Still true to her love of the color, Micheline wore a bright blue, low cut shantung frock that caught and reflected the blue of her eyes.

Lorraine turned her around oohing and aahing, then laughed. They began to chatter like African parrots, their words spilling over like the cold drinks the busy waiters were plying them with.

An hour later, Micheline tapped her friend on the shoulder and declared, "Now that I have assisted at your party, you must assist at mine."

Looking mildly astonished, Lorraine asked, "What? Two receptions in the same evening?"

Eyes twinkling with merriment, Micheline replied, "You get the idea." She drained her glass and deposited it on the tray of a passing waiter.

"Seriously, I cannot miss mine. Today it is July first, Canada's national day, or had you already forgotten?" she said, her blue eyes mocking, as she peered at her friend.

Murmuring soberly and with a slight nod, Lorraine answered, "I had, you know. I guess I'm still jet lagged."

Chuckling, Micheline asked, "Remember the fun we used to have in Montreal on Canada Day when you did not go home for the summer?"

"Do I ever!" Lorraine answered, her eyes suddenly nostalgic.

"But I have one question, Micheline," Lorraine said. "How will I get back to my hotel if I go to your reception?" Micheline gave her a questioning look. Lorraine explained, "My colleagues and I came here in a minivan furnished by the government, with a chauffeur, a Mr. Diop."

"I will drive you. I have my car," her friend declared.

With a little laugh Lorraine replied, "Okay. But I'd better tell Sam or he'll pout like an old woman." Micheline looked perplexed.

Lorraine explained. "He's our scheduling boss on this assignment." She went off to find him.

When Momar arrived at his apartment earlier in the day, he had been too weary to even shower. He had undressed, plopped into bed and slept. He had risen only after his servant had awakened him to ask if he should prepare dinner. Momar had been dreaming, of all things, about the woman on the plane. After dismissing his servant, Momar took a long shower. Dripping water, he moved from the bathroom to the coffee table in the living room, which was piled with mail. Curious, he began to sift through the letters.

"Aha!" he grinned. He had missed the Ministry of Foreign Affairs' reception for the American film crew.

"Fine," he said with all the sarcasm he could muster. He was still smarting from having been assigned to them. His mind returned to the woman on the plane. Perhaps he could have inquired about her at that reception. But he dismissed that thought. Dakar was small, and he already knew she was American. Her accent had betrayed her when she had spoken French with the cabin attendant. Most likely, he had not blown his chance to find out who she was.

Among his mail was another invitation, this one from the Canadian Embassy inviting him to attend their national holiday reception.

"Oh well, might as well go to that," he said without enthusiasm. "At least they speak French," he decided. "Anyway, I am not good company for myself tonight."

The Canadian Embassy residence looked like something that could have made the front page of *House Beautiful* and every other home decorating magazine Lorraine had ever seen, she thought when she saw its white facade. It was set off by a huge, white, wrought iron gate. The brilliantly lit garden was full of roses, birds of paradise and other exotic flowers Lorraine had never seen before. The night was suddenly redolent with the scent of them. They were orange, midnight blue, purple, white…she lost track of the colors as the beds of blossoms gave way to the throng that filled the spaces left by them.

Before she realized it, Micheline was introducing her to someone. "Your Excellency, may I present a friend from my university days in Montreal, Lorraine Barbette." Micheline was shaking hands with the ambassador as she spoke and moving down the reception line.

The Canadian ambassador was a pink-faced, cheerful, slightly chubby man of about fifty. Lorraine smiled as he squeezed her hands in his chubby ones before saying, with that distinct French-Canadian accent she had come to love so much when she lived in Montreal, *"Bonjour, Mademoiselle et soyez la bienvenue."* (Hello, Miss, and welcome.)

Lorraine graciously acknowledged his greeting in his language. She glanced above his balding head and had the urge to curtsy because she found herself staring at a life-size color portrait of Queen Elizabeth and Prince Phillip. She refrained, however, and continued along the reception line, shaking hands and murmuring pleasantries.

Suddenly, the line ended and she and Micheline were plunged into the crowd of international diplomats, local dignitaries, and their spouses, many of whom she recognized as having attended the first reception.

"Lorraine. Lorraine," Micheline had to call her name twice before she heard her. She'd been listening with fascination to the Swiss ambassador and his wife recount their wild boar hunting trips to the northern part of Sénégal, near the Mauritanian border.

She excused herself and turned toward her friend. Micheline's hand rested on the arm of a handsome, well-muscled man who, although in profile, she could see was tall and slim.

He turned at something Micheline said, and a devastating smile split his black face. He was the man she had seen on the plane! Sweat trickled under Lorraine's arms. Someone had lit a fire inside her!

"Lorraine," her friend repeated and she continued in French. "I would like you to meet His Excellency Monsieur Momar Diallo." The man from the airplane held out a long, slender black hand toward her. But Lorraine's brain had gone lame.

She did not take in the details of what he was wearing, just something long and white. When she could focus again, which seemed like a century to her, her gray eyes darted to his face, where they lingered. Under the jet eyebrows, she saw a dark line of curly short lashes that defined those eyes of deep ebony. That much she remembered from the airplane. Light smile lines framed a surprisingly small mouth. The racially unmixed facial structure gave the definitive impression of control, intelligence and a certain savoir faire. It was a face, she decided, that was forged for hope, for endearment, and especially for desire.

His dark eyes left her face, then fell to her neck and further down, admiringly.

Lorraine's sense of excitement swelled.

Momar feasted on her even more boldly than he had in the airplane.

Lorraine was more firmly bewitched than she had ever been in her life. She felt a physical response that had lain dormant for months. His presence was overpowering.

"Whoops. Hey, you two," Micheline said, laughing. "Yoo-hoo," she waved her hand between Lorraine and Momar. "I am still here. Remember me?"

Lorraine was the first to recover. "Er, er, yes, *monsieur...*?"

"Diallo," he supplied, still holding her hand. His touch seemed to burn her.

She did not want to let go of him, afraid she would not be able to stand alone. She used the excuse of taking a drink from one of the waiters, steadied herself, and sipped her drink to cool down. She could not trust her voice.

Micheline, recognizing that she was no longer necessary, discreetly withdrew.

"I noticed you the minute you arrived, Miss Barbette. You were on the flight from New York," Momar told Lorraine. After Micheline had gone, their conversation continued in French.

"Yes," she breathed, nearly suffocating, her voice a whisper. She heard nothing else he said until, as though through a fog, he was saying, "I am fascinated by you African-Americans."

Suddenly wary, she asked more sharply than she intended, "What's fascinating about African-Americans that's not fascinating about other Americans?"

Ignoring the sudden chill in her voice, he said, "You have a chance to come home to Africa, but in spite of the way you are treated in America, you stay there," he added smugly, she thought.

Lorraine's gray eyes glowered. She replied, deadly serious, "I don't know what you know about the United

States or about African-Americans, Monsieur Diallo, but I have to assume your information is second hand and therefore not necessarily correct."

That should fix his smug attitude, she thought.

But Diallo merely gazed, transfixed, at Lorraine. Nevertheless, sensing her seriousness, he leaned forward, touched her elbow, his voice intense, low. "I really and sincerely would like to get to know you better, Miss Barbette. Perhaps then you could educate me about the plight of my cousins in America. I was not there long enough to learn as much as I would have liked to."

Lorraine did not know whether he was being serious or not and became even more wary. She was hesitant to reply. She became aware of the hum of conversation around them. In the silence that rested between them, she finally said in a rush, "I find the heat in here overwhelming, Monsieur Diallo. Do you mind?" She began edging toward the back of the room.

Suddenly she felt like swooning. But was it from jet lag, Africa, or this man? she asked herself, silently, suddenly panicky. She had to escape. She turned quickly, almost colliding with several people.

Staring at the space she had so recently vacated, Momar could still smell her Chanel 19 perfume. He swore softly. "*Zut!* I have blown it now. I said all the wrong things. She will never speak to me again."

He had not believed his eyes when he had spotted her among the crowd as soon as he'd arrived at the reception. And now to have met her officially only to lose her…"Some diplomat you are," he chided himself sarcastically.

"Damn it man, go after her," he told himself, oblivious to the quick, curious glances as several heads turned and eyes gawked in his wake. He strode toward the French doors.

Lorraine stepped into the relatively cool air and found herself on a dimly lit patio, surrounded by blossoming orange trees set in huge white wooden buckets. The fragrance was overwhelming, heady.

"Hello again," Momar said, this time in perfect English. His teeth gleamed against his black skin.

In a low, strained voice, Lorraine asked, "How did you know where to find me?" Her heart was thumping so loud she was sure he could hear it.

"I watched you. That is how," he said as he moved toward her. "Why did you leave the reception? Did I say something to offend you?" He leaned forward, a peculiar searching look on his face.

Fighting to keep her voice steady, she replied. "No. I really don't like crowds, and I suddenly felt…faint." She hoped that simple answer would satisfy him because she was afraid she was going to swoon and fall into his arms if he remained standing before her. His slim, elegantly clad body was outlined against the light from the room where the reception was going on.

Momar, his voice husky with emotion, blurted, "I had to see you again."

Lorraine inhaled the heavily scented orange blossoms, now mixed with his tangy after-shave lotion, and sighed deeply to keep from swooning. She could feel the strong magnetic force of his body drawing her toward him. Is this what Africa does to one? she wondered, terrified at what she felt like doing.

"Won't your party be wondering about your absence?" she asked, her voice wobbly, but husky and very low.

"No. They are occupied," he replied, moving even closer to her.

Foolishly, she felt a flow of guilty happiness and contentment. But this was ridiculous; she'd only just met this man. "What brought you to Sénégal?" asked Momar in a low whisper. He leaned against the patio wall, swirling his drink with a casual air he was far from feeling.

"I, I'm, I'm here to, to work..." she stammered, her voice shaking in spite of herself. He was somewhat reassured to realize that she was as nervous as he was and that she would be in Sénégal for awhile.

"How about you?" she asked. Although she already knew the answer, Lorraine wanted to hear his lilting speech. She asked again, "How about you?" Her slim white dress rustled from a small breeze and sounded like thunder in her ears.

In a barely audible voice, he murmured, "I am with the Foreign Office."

"You speak English beautifully," she whispered.

"And you speak French beautifully," he replied, with a flashing eye. He admitted, "I overheard you talking in the plane with the cabin attendant."

"You were eavesdropping!" she accused, admiring his lithe, yet powerful body outlined against the reception room light.

And she believed he wouldn't remember having seen her, she thought, delighted that he'd been interested enough to eavesdrop on her conversation.

The emotion she felt was so heady that she leaned against the patio wall for support.

Placing the empty wine glass in the branches of one of the potted orange trees, Momar caressed the hair at the side of her neck. He had wanted to do that since their flight. His hand caressed the smoothness of her face, moving down to her slender neck.

He leaned toward her, and she could feel him trembling throughout his body. Her own body trembled, too, and she felt like a drum somebody had hit very hard. She turned her willing mouth to him and he took it, easily. His warm, soft lips touched hers in a sweetly seductive kiss.

She felt his body responding as she released her passions. His strong, powerful form moved closer and pressed against her, first gently, then more demandingly. She reacted in kind, allowing the kiss to deepen, no longer thinking or caring, just knowing that she needed what she was accepting from this man she had only met formally a few moments ago. A man she knew hardly anything about. Only what he and Micheline had told her so briefly.

"No!" She could not believe it was her voice, croaking out a strangled, "No. No."

He released her abruptly.

Feeling numb and a bit dizzy, she took a step away from him.

There was a long, crackling silence. Finally, Momar broke it. "I thought you wanted to be kissed," he said quietly, watching her. "I have wanted to do that since I first saw you," he added.

"Well, I, I…" Lorraine stammered, faintly. She moved as far as she was capable in her shaky state.

"I must see you again," Momar growled thickly. Gazing at her intently, he asked in a low voice, "When may I see you? Will you have lunch with me tomorrow?"

"I can't. I'm having lunch with Micheline," she lied weakly, still shaking.

"Then dinner," he insisted.

"We had better return to the reception," she said, edging toward the open French doors. She was afraid of what she would do if she stayed another minute alone with him. She found Micheline surrounded by a crowd of admirers. She introduced everyone to Lorraine, who did not retain a single name. Afterward, on the drive back to her hotel, Lorraine sat tensely in the passenger side of her friend's low-slung sports car.

Finally, to break the silence and above the quiet hum of the car, Lorraine asked, hesitantly, choosing her words carefully, "Micheline, how long will Mr. Diallo be in Dakar? Do you know?"

"He is on leave. As far as I know, he is waiting for a new posting. He could be here for months and then again, he could be reassigned tomorrow," the other woman replied truthfully. She took her eyes off the road momentarily to gaze at her friend.

"Why do you ask?"

"I…just wondered," Lorraine hedged, lying.

Micheline did not look fooled, but she said nothing.

They drove in silence for the rest of the way, and when they arrived at Lorraine's hotel she thanked her friend profusely. They pecked each other on the cheeks, then Lorraine glided from the car, up the stairs and out of sight.

She did not see the worried look creeping into her friend's lovely blue eyes before she drove away.

3

After a nearly sleepless night, Lorraine was awake when the last high note of the meuzzin's call to prayers melted into silence. She kept mulling over what Micheline had told her about Momar. Her thoughts ran amok with nagging questions. Lorraine was thinking with her heart. Her mind churned. Memories of Momar flitted through her head. Something had indefinably changed.

She knew that she had been right to insist on coming to Sénégal. Again, she had the strong feeling that this, now and here, was a turning point in her life. She had a feeling about this assignment and about this place, about life.

Daylight broke suddenly into a stunning brightness. Lorraine stretched, turned on the radio and slid from the bed. She padded into the bathroom with a motion that cats practice years to perfect. "My first overseas assignment," she crooned, hugging herself, delirious at the thought.

Under the soothing warm spray of the shower, Lorraine allowed her mind to return to the unpleasant meeting with her ex-fiancé back in Mississippi.

She remembered her excitement when her boss, Stanton Carter, had confirmed that she'd been selected for the assignment in Sénégal. From New York she'd booked the first seat available to Memphis, the closest airport to Mound Bayou.

She remembered telephoning her parents and grand-parents right away with the good news. They were all ecstatic and congratulated her profusely. She had purpose-fully asked all of them to not tell Andrew. She wanted to tell him herself, thinking he'd be just as happy for her.

It had been a terrible mistake. Lorraine felt saddened that their long relationship ended the way it did. After all, they had known each other all their lives.

Andrew Kemp did have some good qualities: he was good looking in a serious way, and he was kind, when he wanted to be. But mostly, Andrew was a man who knew exactly where he was going and what he wanted to do. He became principal of the school, and he would become mayor of Mound Bayou one day; that was certain.

Lorraine had come to realize, however, that his quest for power and control had gotten worse over time.

She bet he controlled his students just like he wanted to control her. But she would never let him control her. She'd finally made up her mind, once and for all. The engage-ment was over, but when she returned from Sénégal, she hoped they could again, at least, be friends.

She would never forget Andrew or her years growing up in Mound Bayou. She remembered standing with her cousins on her grandmother's front porch, all dresses starched, shoes polished and gay hair ribbons. In fact, such a scene was her earliest memory. She was three years old and waiting for her mother to arrive from town and claim her. After a summer in the country, the very young Lorraine had actually forgotten what her mother looked like and was a bit shy when the elegant lady drove up.

From her earliest childhood she had spent the summers, and any other time she could, with her maternal grandmother, who was half Choctaw Indian.

What Lorraine liked most was the forest, which fronted her grandparent's property. Every season her grandmother would take her into the forest. In the spring they found fresh green plants and tender roots. In the summer, they picked various berries, medicinal leaves, roots and flowers. Her grandmother taught her to read dirt patterns and trails, to interpret crushed leaves, to track animals and to catch wild fowl.

In the autumn they picked nuts and hunted with sticks. Her grandmother taught her to kill wild rabbits and squirrels with a foot long round stick. Lorraine did not like to kill wild animals, but she loved to please her grandmother. Her grandmother was her favorite person.

Her mind went to her nursery school when she was five and the wonderful teacher who taught her charges to sing. It was her first contact with the French language, and she fell in love with it.

All through high school she studied French and at the private downstate school where she had graduated with the highest consistent grades in the school's history, she knew that she wanted to study French abroad and make films.

She was ecstatic when Concordia University in Montreal accepted her, and offered her a scholarship to boot.

She remembered running to the telephone to call her beloved grandmother with the good news. Her grandmother had yelled, "Thank you, Jesus!"

Only after talking with her grandmother did she tell her mom and dad. They both were pleased for her, but a bit worried about her going so far away.

Then she told Andrew. He became so angry, she remembered with a shudder. She reminded him then that he didn't own her, but he had rejoined with, "Yes, but you know our families expect us to marry." She enjoyed the five years she spent in Montreal. What a city. What people. What a place, Quebec.

She only returned home for the first two summers. After that she convinced her parents to allow her to visit the province with her friend, Micheline Martin. They had taken turns driving everywhere in the province of Quebec, experiencing its villages, mountains, rivers, people and food. Sometimes they camped, other times they splurged and stayed at the elegant Chateau Frontenac when they visited Quebec City.

Then there was the Island of Orleans! Lorraine recalled happily as she continued rinsing off in the shower. She always remembered the Island of Orleans with an exclamation point. It must be what parts of France are like, she mused.

"My goodness! I've been in this shower too long!" she exclaimed, realizing with a shock that there was no more hot water.

A short time later she decided to order breakfast from room service. She still had some work she wanted to go over before going to the office they were using at the American Embassy.

When she had finished giving her order, she spread her work on the desktop, but her mind kept wandering back to the night before. That patio scene had caught her off guard, but Lorraine felt she had carried off the rest of the evening with composure. However, she had to admit that today she was caught up in a web of terrible conflicting and confusing desires.

Every time she thought about Momar her heart beat like the drums she had seen at the hotel's entertainment. When she thought about Andrew she became angry but felt nothing else.

Breakfast was a blur. Working away in a daze, time slipped away. When she looked at her watch again it was half past nine. She blinked in thought a moment, then dialed the front desk.

"Hello. Hello." She gave her room number and asked in an urgent voice, speaking rapidly in French, "Would you order a taxi for me, please?"

The night before, she, Sam, and Mark had all agreed that they could use the minivan and she would take a taxi to the office this morning. "Yes, *mademoiselle*. Right away, *mademoiselle*," a cheerful desk clerk replied.

Instead of returning to her desk, Lorraine glanced out the window and was surprised to see that a storm was fast brewing. She hastily gathered her papers, stuffed them into her briefcase, checked her purse and hurried to the lobby. Arriving there, she was shocked to see that outside the window, the clouds had already thickened so much they blurred the horizon.

The clerk, noticing her look of concern, spoke up.

"Is this the first time you have been in Sénégal during *hivernage?*"

"*Hivernage?*" She asked, puzzled. She brushed a lock of hair out of her eyes.

"Yes, it is our rainy season," he explained, coming from behind the desk to gaze at the storm.

"But the sky was so clear earlier this morning," Lorraine protested, waving a slender hand towards the lowering gray clouds as though the gesture would make them disappear.

"That is what *hivernage* is like, *mademoiselle.* Sudden rain squalls," he added, strolling to the double doors, looking out.

"Will it last long?" she asked unhappily.

"Sometimes it is over in a matter of minutes. Sometimes it lasts for more than twenty-four hours," he answered. Lorraine's heart sank. The taxi had not yet arrived, and she was going to be terribly late.

"Look," she said, trying not to sound irritable. She glanced at her watch again. "The taxi is slow."

"They have all gone to Yoff Airport because there is a flight coming in," the clerk said. At Lorraine's angry look, he hastened to add, "But I was sure one or maybe two would be back by now."

"Do you have a car I can rent?"

Glad for a way out, the clerk wagged his head in the affirmative and scurried back behind the desk, dialed a number and said something in a language Lorraine did not know. Almost before he had hung up the telephone, a light blue Simca sedan appeared at the front of the hotel.

"Merci," Lorraine called over her shoulder as she ran out the door and down the steps after having completed the rental formalities.

A few minutes later she was squinting through the rippling films of water rolling down the windshield. The wipers of the tiny French car were fighting a losing battle, she realized gloomily as she peered miserably through the downpour.

Momar frowned into his mirror and grimaced at his bloodshot eyes. He had not slept a wink. He wondered what had gotten into him last night. He had acted like a hick. "Miss Barbette must think I am an uncivilized boor," he grimaced again. She was not even his type. "I do not even like tall, thin, 'string bean' women," he laughed, not even convincing himself.

She has a nice figure, he decided grudgingly, remembering their time on the patio. And she has very expressive gray eyes. He noticed that back in the airplane during the flight over. "No, Miss Lorraine Barbette just is not my type," he repeated, trying, but failing to put more emphasis in his declaration.

"If that is so, why did you not sleep at all last night?" came the whisper in his brain. "Why has she been entering and re-entering your thoughts ever since you saw her on the airplane?" The question gnawed at his mind like a dog teasing a bone.

He grimaced as he nicked his face with his razor. His feelings were too dangerous, especially if Lorraine Barbette turned out to be in Sénégal only for a quick fling. An icy thought slipped through the base of his mind. Suppose she was here for only a few days before going on to other African countries. He had seen countless African-Americans who were "touring Africa." He fervently hoped that was not true in her case. She had said that she was working. Must be with one of the agencies or maybe with her embassy, he decided.

Momar finished his toilette, dressed and ate a hasty breakfast, which he did not taste. "Do not prepare lunch for me, Samba." he told his servant. "I have a date with the delegation from the Ivorian Foreign Ministry. We will be at La Tonkinoise if anyone telephones and it is urgent."

"Yes, sir," his servant acknowledged and was about to close the door when Momar remembered the hateful American assignment, as he had dubbed it.

"And, Samba, I go directly to the Ministry of Information after lunch."

"Very well, sir."

"That's enough for now, Lorraine, Mark. The rain has let up. Let's find something to eat," Sam Benson said, hitching up his slightly baggy pants.

"Okay by me," Mark answered, standing up too. He gave a loud yawn and stretched. "We've covered a lot of ground this morning. We know where we want to begin filming if the Senegalese officials agree," he added.

"Let me finish this last sentence," Lorraine said, reaching for a fresh sheet of paper. "And don't forget that I have to approve and direct everything we do here," she reminded the two men.

"Yes ma'am. We know you're the producer and director, Ms. Barbette," Mark said, laughing and bowing with a Three Musketeers flourish.

They all laughed.

A few moments later, Sam said, holding the heavy opaque glass door for Lorraine and Mark, "Someone here told me that there's a great restaurant near here called La Tonkinoise."

His two colleagues edged around him and out the door without comment. "That doesn't sound African to me," Mark said once they were outside.

"Probably isn't," Sam answered. "This city is more international than New York. You could be anywhere in the world," he commented as they turned the corner into Boulevard de la Republique. Abruptly all three stopped as if they had walked into a glass wall.

"Do you see what I see?" Lorraine exclaimed, the first to recover. She stared dumbfounded from Mark to Sam then back to the breathtaking sight. Both men were gaping, their mouths open wide.

"Damn it!" Mark yelled. "Why did I leave my camera at the embassy?"

"Because you lack the professional touch," Lorraine answered, her gray eyes mirthful.

Sam added in awe, "Nobody back home will ever believe this. That's the biggest, sharpest, darn rainbow you have ever seen, I bet."

"They don't make 'em that beautiful even back in Mississippi," Lorraine quipped. "Just look at all those colors: red, orange, yellow, green, blue, indigo, violet! I'm seeing it, but I don't believe it!"

"Make a wish quickly because we're going to walk right through it!" Mark exclaimed, as excited as a small child who had just found his Christmas wish under the tree on Christmas morning.

"Let me at the pot of gold!" Lorraine cried and sprinted so quickly that her leather-soled sandals skidded on the rain slick pavement.

They were still flushed with excitement at having seen the blazing colors arched across the sky when they reached the restaurant.

Lorraine was slightly disappointed that the restaurant did not have outdoor seating but she did not say anything. She just wanted to savor the blazing colors of the rainbow awhile longer.

Sam told the Asian-African waiter who met them at the entrance that someone at the embassy had made reservations for them.

The waiter grinned and bowed them to their table. Interested eyes followed their progress and a slight hush descended at each table as they passed.

Lorraine was impressed with the dining room of La Tonkinoise. They could have been in the South Seas. The walls were tastefully decorated with fish netting, artistically draped with giant seashells, starfish, and seaweed. Colorful Japanese lanterns hung from the ceiling. Huge potted palms were placed in a manner to give each table, which held a bouquet of fresh flowers, a measure of intimacy.

That is why Lorraine did not see Momar and the people sitting at his table until she had sat down and looked around the restaurant. "I said, do you want an aperitif, Lorraine? I don't believe you've heard a thing I said," Sam grumbled.

"Sorry," Lorraine blinked, hoping the light was too poor for her companions to see the sudden tears in her eyes. "Ah, no. I don't think I'll have an aperitif. But you both go ahead, though."

Lorraine could see that Momar was in an animated conversation with an exquisitely beautiful Afro-Asian woman who seemed to hang on his every word.

The woman's elegant looks made Lorraine aware of her comparatively dull, dark striped dress, but then again it did match her sudden change of mood. She could not keep her eyes away from the table where Momar was dining. Oblivious to the admiring stares directed her way, Lorraine was filled with longing only for the man across the room.

He appeared at ease, full of geniality and charm, a sophisticated urbane man of the world, enjoying the company of the people in his party.

After she had ordered lunch, Lorraine tried to study him dispassionately while Sam and Mark talked shop, but she found Momar's presence too disturbing.

She began to long for the closed and known dimensions of her past life. *What am I doing here on the other side of the world anyway, away from my home? Away from my people? Away from everything I know?* she thought to herself in a moment of deep pessimism.

Lorraine felt foolish for allowing Momar to kiss her. "If only I had it to do over, I would react differently," she whispered too low for her companions to hear. She was now ashamed of her rash loss of control and wondered if it showed. But Sam Benson, with his usual smug, dominating air, was not paying attention to her. Instead he had gotten Mark into an argument about their filming schedule.

When the waiter came to clear away their plates, he noticed that Lorraine had hardly touched her food. "The food is not to mademoiselle's liking?" He asked, hovering, his face showing concern.

Sam and Mark seemed to notice only then that she had not eaten. Mark, his face puzzled and concerned, said, "Are you all right? You hardly touched your food."

Seeing Momar so engrossed in his table companion had marred Lorraine's day, but she attempted to keep her sadness at bay when she answered in a voice devoid of expression, "I know. I guess I'm just not hungry after all."

"You should have had an aperitif," pronounced Sam.

"Maybe I should have. I'll have a glass of white wine," she said in a casual tone, hoping that would satisfy Sam.

Momar was relieved to be free of that Ivorian delegation.

He had barely enough diplomatic patience to put up with the Ivorian's gloating over what they considered Abidjan's winning the tourist rivalry with Dakar. The lunch could have been a pleasant one if he had not been forced to listen to the three of them list Abidjan's tourist advantages. And that Miss whatever-her-name, parroting the tourist advertisements: "Can you imagine, Monsieur Diallo! We have the only indoor ice skating rink in all of Africa!"

The woman gazed at Momar as if she expected him to agree with her, he remembered as he stalked along to the ministry for his new assignment.

"I felt like telling her that it was a travesty since some people were without enough food to eat," he spoke aloud, causing several people to turn and stare at him. He did not care. He was angry. "And that other chap, whatever-his-name—was, chiming in with his snideness: 'When does Sénégal intend to install commercial television, Monsieur Diallo?' "

Momar was surprised he had been able to hold his lunch. They made him sick to his stomach. *"Zut!"* He spat at the memory of that terrible luncheon.

He was in no mood to meet the Minister of Information's deputy and accept another "assignment." He slackened his stride in order to give himself time to simmer down.

By the time the crowded elevator reached the floor he wanted, he was relatively calm.

"Oh, Monsieur Diallo, the minister's deputy is expecting you." The young, extravagantly dressed secretary gushed at him as soon as he stepped into her crowded office. With that she minced across the room on dangerously high-heeled shoes and tapped loudly at an inner door. She opened it before the loud, "Come in!" boomed out, then stepped aside as he entered.

Moustapha Ba, Deputy Minister of Information, took his position seriously. Thus, when the Minister of Foreign

Affairs himself had telephoned to confirm that Momar Diallo would help with that American film crew, the deputy was effusive in his elation.

Now, he jumped to his feet, coming quickly from behind his untidy desk, and began pumping Momar's hand in greeting while a huge grin split his dark face.

"Sit down, man. You look great. By the way, my belated condolences on your loss. How was America? Heard about Sall. What a pity. A bad name for Sénégal." His sentences were running together. He was not giving the younger man time to say a word. So Momar gingerly removed a pile of papers from a chair and sat down.

Ba finally came to a verbal stop and returned to his chair behind his desk.

"Thank you for your condolences, but it has been six months now, Ba, since my wife died. I did not see much of America. I am here about the assignment," Momar replied succinctly, hoping he wasn't being rude.

"Yes, of course," the deputy acknowledged, shuffling a pile of papers. "Ah, here we are," he cried triumphantly, holding up a bunch of wrinkled papers as though they were a trophy.

"Let us see," he said, peering at the papers. "Your Americans are working at their embassy. Their guide and chauffeur is Mansour Diop." He stopped and looked expectantly at Momar, who made no sign he was listening.

"You are to meet them at the embassy tomorrow morning. By the way, the two other members of our diplomatic team, Badoye Koha and Aminata Baumé, will be with you."

Momar was pleased to be working again with Aminata. She was a good person with whom he'd worked before. He spoke for the first time since Ba had begun his report. "Allah be praised. I do not have to face those people alone."

"I take it Americans are not your favorite people?" Ba smiled.

"You remember the film crew that was here last year, do you not?" Momar asked, instead of answering.

"Yes. I see what you mean. Well, this time there are three of you and three of them. They have one woman and two men, and so do you. So, if they show signs of getting out of hand, you are evenly matched." Deputy Minister Ba chuckled at his own wit.

"You sound as if you do not quite trust them either, Ba. What are they supposed to be filming?"

"According to the papers they filed with us, they want to film 'cultural activities.' You and I know with foreigners that could mean anything."

Did he indeed. He remembered other foreign film crews. After a few more pleasantries Momar took his leave.

Lorraine, who had worked away the rest of the day, rooted through her handbag for her car keys. Momar's kiss had engraved itself upon her mind, but she could not forget the scene in the restaurant. She had a stranded, left-behind kind of feeling that lingered no matter how hard she tried to make it go away.

She used to dream of coming to Africa, and now that she was here, she felt caught up in a crazy web of new feelings and desires. She opened her borrowed umbrella and stepped gingerly out into the new downpour. She still felt an echo of humiliation. Lorraine felt she had been a good actress in the restaurant in spite of the tightness that still lingered in her stomach.

The twilight hour and the rain had converged on Dakar like a soft shawl drawn over its stone shoulders as Lorraine eased out the clutch of her rented Simca. As she pulled out into the clogged streets, the rain beating on the car roof, she kept mulling over what Micheline had told her about Momar. The man could be posted anywhere at anytime. Yet Lorraine could not escape the feeling that she was at a preordained, mystic junction in her life and that the attractive African man was somehow a part of it.

She surveyed this strange city as she drove, watching the people restlessly as they went about their business despite the downpour. Communal taxis, car rapides, minibuses with passengers hanging precariously on the sides and backs, private cars, carts, bicycles and mopeds all whizzed around her car. Huge throngs of people jammed the sidewalks. "This is rush hour, Dakar style," she laughed above the noise of the rain and turned up the car radio.

As she neared her hotel, the rain was still pounding the car windows, roof and hood. Jagged lightening flickered against the sky to the west, followed by heavy thunder that rumbled like a thousand tomtoms.

Quarter-sized drops fell around Lorraine as she ran from her car to the shelter of the hotel door. By the time she reached it, her dress clung to her body like a second skin. Her sandals were ruined and her hair was plastered to her head. She had never seen rain go through an umbrella as though it did not exist.

As she let herself into her hotel room, she felt very lost and lonely. Quickly she shed her soaking dress and undergarments. Instinctively she knew this assignment was a valuable and exciting opportunity. The next few weeks would determine the rest of her life. But for now, her mood matched the weather outside. Stormy.

Because her head was as clogged as her mind the next morning, she bowed out of the optional meeting. Sam and Mark would meet the Senegalese group that was to be their escort for the filming near Ziguinchor. She would settle down and catch up on her research.

4

When Lorraine reported for work again, Sam Benson called a meeting to acquaint them with their scheduling around Dakar.

Everyone was seated in the office he was using in the information section at the American Embassy, and he began. "In a few weeks, people, we'll be the most famous film company in the Good Ole U. S. of A." He hooked his thumbs in his vest armholes and leaned expansively back with a smug expression on his pudgy face. His eyes ranged from face to face of his assembled crew.

Lorraine broke the silence. "We're going to be famous making cultural films?"

"Yep. The kind of cultural films we'll be making after we finish filming in Sénégal's Saint Louis."

"Sam," Mark spoke up, "I think we have a right to know our full schedule as soon as possible."

"Why?" Sam asked, piercing Mark with a steely glare.

"Because I've brought along the film we'll need for what was scheduled, but if we're going to be doing something more, I'll have to order extra film now."

"Hold your horses, Whitman. You got special film for night filming, haven't you?" Sam asked.

"Well, yes, but I don't think we'll need too much of that."

"I'll decide that," Sam snapped, reminding them that he was the scheduling boss.

"Let me remind both of you," he said, his eyes shooting from Lorraine to Mark, "Cultural Sights and Sounds is paying high enough wages that I can think of a hundred cameramen who would give their eyeteeth to work for us. No questions asked."

"Is that a threat?" Mark asked.

"Look, both of you," Lorraine jumped in, "I'm the producer and director of this project. Sam, you know as well as I that a detailed schedule is absolutely necessary if we're to work efficiently," Lorraine reminded them.

"I'll have a detailed schedule at our next meeting but till then, use the one I filed with the Ministry of Information," Sam snapped, refusing to give an inch.

"This is strictly a cultural affair, isn't it?" Lorraine asked, then added for emphasis, "I only do cultural films."

"Don't worry," was all she could get out of Sam.

Lorraine and Mark, knowing the meeting was over, were headed for the door when Sam threw at them, as an afterthought, "Oh, by the way, don't forget there is a group of three Senegalese people who will be our official escort when we film near Ziguinchor."

Lorraine headed for her embassy office, reviewing the meeting in her head. She had more questions than answers. She knew no more about their schedule than she had before. And what did Sam mean about this cultural film on Sénégal making them rich and famous? She reviewed what she knew about the country. Everything she could come up with had already been filmed and documented. As a matter of fact, she was going to have to come up with some very original story lines so that Cultural Sights and Sounds could sell the films.

Surely this was just one more example of Sam's bragging. By revealing as few details as possible he could retain the feeling of power. That was one of the things she had always disliked about working with him. He worked by the seat of his pants and was not a team player by any stretch.

As the tedious days wore on, Lorraine's routine did not vary. Up early, work, home, to bed exhausted, which, of course, did not help her confused state. Most of the time she felt like an unwound clock.

She was nearly finished retyping a clean copy of one of her direction scripts for the shoot to be done in Saint Louis. Her wastepaper basket was overflowing. A thin film of moisture formed on her upper lip.

"Damn!" she hissed, furious that there wasn't a computer she could use. This old typewriter had given her nothing but trouble. Another line of mistakes, and she was tearing the half-finished sheet from her typewriter.

"Lorraine." Hearing her name, she whirled to face Wilson Graves, their liaison for this mission and the information officer at the embassy.

"Yes, Mr. Graves," Lorraine answered warily, waiting for him to continue. He was an oddly built man of about fifty-five. His smug manner had nettled her from the first time she had met him.

Graves spoke curtly, his drawl betraying his origins as the American South. "There is a press conference over at the presidential palace in an hour. You'll have to cover it. I'll give you all the particulars you need and supply a car and chauffeur for you."

Lorraine studied him coldly. "I'm not a reporter, Mr. Graves, and I don't work for you." Then she turned to feed more paper into her machine.

Graves, his mouth agape, sputtered, "Give you people an inch and you take a mile. I just told you, there is no one else here. You must cover that press conference. That's an order, not a request!"

Lorraine whipped around to face him again, slammed her hand down on the desk so hard that papers there did a little dance. "Mister Graves, I don't think you heard me correctly," she began icily. "I don't work for you. Just because we use an office in your section of the embassy and you're our liaison officer doesn't give *you* the right to *order* any of us around. Give you an inch and you take a mile," she said.

"But, but," he sputtered, "there's a delegation from the Ivory Coast. There is nobody else here who speaks enough French…" His voice trailed off as his face competed in color with her bright red typewriter.

Glaring into his face, she said with as much authority as she could, "That is not my problem, and it has nothing to do with me. Now, if you will excuse me, I have my own work to finish." She turned to her typewriter.

He said shortly, "You people are all alike. Never grateful when someone tries to help you out."

Lorraine whipped around again, giving him an icy gray stare that took in his broad nose and thick brows. His bloodshot eyes added to the harshness of his features. His florid hue, short, receding gray hair and well-developed paunch testified to how he was passing his unhappy assignment time. She had heard that he over-bossed his staff and she knew he was a Southerner by his accent. She had heard the Senegalese staff complaining that he disliked blacks.

In a voice that could have frozen molten iron, she finally spat out, *"Mister* Graves, I fail to see how my covering a press conference that has nothing to do with me or my work is 'helping me out' as you put it. I arrived here with my own assignment, which has nothing to do with your press conference." He gaped again. She observed that he had a habit of looking like a frightened frog.

She went on, her icy gray eyes sharp and direct. "As for being 'grateful', I don't know what you're talking about. Now, if you'll excuse me, I have something else to do. Good day!"

His stereotypical outlook and his manner made her fume. Was he so thick-witted as to think that just because she typed she had to run his errands?

To show him that he was dismissed, she picked up the telephone on her desk, dialed nine to get an outside line and furiously dialed Micheline's private line at the Canadian Embassy. She whirled her chair around, placing her back to Wilson Graves. She heard a ring on the other end.

When Micheline answered, Lorraine spoke quickly, "Micheline, Lorraine here. Are you free for lunch?"

"Hi, there," Micheline answered cheerfully. "I was beginning to think you had returned home without letting me know. Lunch? Today? Sure thing. Where?"

"You know the places here better than I do. You name it and I'll find it."

"Fine. Meet me at the restaurant in the Hotel Teranga in half an hour. That is easy to find. It is in the center of town and the food is good, for a hotel."

"Okay." She rang off.

When Lorraine turned her chair around, Wilson Graves had gone.

Lorraine had gotten used to Dakar with its bustling style and distinct aromas. As she drove along Boulevard de la Republique, cars flashed past her under branches of the low-hanging, brightly blossoming flame trees. She drove past prosperous-looking, former European homes, past the white-washed, rambling structures. *These are peculiar people,* she mused, *these Senegalese, not at all what I expected.*

When she drew near a knot of people, she saw they were pressing in on a hapless pedestrian who had lost to a fast Dakar driver. "Poor chap," she sighed. She slowed down but did not stop since the policeman, standing in the center of the street, was screaming and flapping his arms at the traffic and at the people pressing in on the pedestrian, who didn't seem to be too badly hurt.

A few moments later, Micheline called from across the parking lot, "You hoo, Lorraine! I am over here." Lorraine left her car. They met midway, hugged, pecked each other on the cheek and stood back to mutually admire each other. "That white linen suit really makes you look super,"

Micheline said, turning her friend around. "You look as cool as the proverbial cucumber," she said admiringly.

"I'm just the opposite," Lorraine said. "I'm as hot as a smoking pistol."

"Oh, come on. What is up?" Her friend, realizing she was serious, took her hand companionably as they walked towards the hotel.

The maître d', Souleymane, standing at the entrance to the hotel restaurant, was dressed somberly in a black suit with a fluffy white shirt and gleaming white teeth. His cherub black eyes lit up when he saw Micheline and Lorraine.

"Bonjour, mademoiselles," he bowed. "What an honor you pay us. Two?" He asked, glancing appreciatively at Lorraine.

"Yes, Souley. Two of your best seats," Micheline grinned, following him. Lorraine brought up the rear. The restaurant was crowded with the noonday crowd of tourists, diplomats and downtown government officials. When they had been seated, Souley asked if they wanted an aperitif. "I need one," Lorraine sighed. "You can't imagine what I've just been through." She rolled her eyes at Micheline.

"I will have a gin and tonic," Micheline decided. "And what will you have, Lorraine?"

"A vodka martini," she answered. Then asked the maitre d', "do you have that?"

Souleymane, who was very proud of his bar, bowed, smiling.

"Souley," Micheline asked, "have the wine steward come over, please."

"Oui, mademoiselle," he flashed another grin and left them. Once the maitre d' had gone, Micheline placed both hands on the table and said, "Now tell me what happened."

Lorraine recounted her run-in with Wilson Graves.

"Whew! That is a hot one," the Canadian woman cried when her friend finished.

Their drinks had arrived and Lorraine, picking up her glass, said, "Let's forget the Wilson Graves of this world. What have you been doing since we last saw each other?"

Micheline's blue eyes became mischievous as she clicked her glass with Lorraine's, took a sip of her drink, and said dreamily, "I have just met this super diplomat from Germany."

The wine steward arrived. Micheline took the wine list and he withdrew. Before they could take another sip of their drinks, the chef appeared.

"Miss Micheline, I thought I saw you come in," he said, beaming, his high white chef's hat sitting atop his round black head like a bleached basketball. His white suit and apron made him look like a tropical Santa. Micheline accepted the peck on the cheek he quickly planted while he held onto his high chef's hat.

"What would you ladies like to order?" he asked, eyeing Lorraine but directing his words to Micheline.

"What do you suggest today, Ousseynou?" Lorraine could see the chef was flattered when Micheline asked for his suggestions. He tipped back on his heels and proudly began to recite the day's menu.

"Hold it. Would somebody explain? I haven't the slightest notion what all of this is about," Lorraine exclaimed, holding up her hands in mock defense.

"Bassi salete is the local couscous served with meat or fish, *mademoiselle. Yassa* is rice with marinated onions, spices, and chicken. *Chebbou yapp* is meat and rice."

"I like the sound of them all!" Lorraine said, laughing again.

"What do you want, then?" Micheline asked, smiling at her friend's excitement.

"Yassa. That sounds wonderful," Lorraine clapped her hands. "It is spicy, mademoiselle," Ousseynou warned.

"I love spicy food," Lorraine told him and grinned again.

"I am going to have…*yassa,* too," Micheline finally decided. Looking pleased, Ousseynou bowed and left them. Lorraine glanced around the restaurant at the richly-colored upholstery on the plush chairs and the tables with their matching cloths. Each one had a vase of exotic African flowers in its center. The walls were lined with paintings of Senegalese scenes and murals with jungle motifs. The carpet was thick enough to mute the sound of conversation and clinking silverware.

"Oh, by the way, Micheline," Lorraine leaned forward, choosing her words carefully, "I saw your friend, Mr. Diallo, at a restaurant last week."

"He gets around a lot," Micheline said with a sudden laugh. "After all, he is on leave."

Just the sound of his name gave Lorraine an odd, heady feeling. A queer passion welled up in her. She was glad the wine steward claimed their attention.

"I suggest we try the *Boulaoune,* Lorraine, if that is all right with you," Micheline said, unaware of her friend's disarmed state. Lorraine sipped her vodka and nodded her head, glad she did not have to answer. "Now what have you been doing that I have not seen you all week?" Micheline queried expectantly.

"I've been working on our scripts for the Saint Louis filming. But I'm almost finished with them. We're to work there in two weeks time."

"If you have all that time, why you must come with me. I am going to Saint Louis the day after tomorrow. It will give you a chance to scout around before your filming begins," Micheline said. "Now, that makes it seem as if I know something about your work, does it not?" Both women laughed.

Then Lorraine replied, "You're right, I suppose I could…" She sounded uncertain.

"Oh, do say yes," Micheline urged, eyeing her glass before taking another sip of her drink.

"Okay. Why not," Lorraine agreed. They clinked glasses to seal the deal, then began excitedly discussing the details.

The meals arrived. Between bites of food and sips of wine, they discussed their careers, their days in Quebec. They recalled their escapades at the annual Quebec Winter Carnival.

Each time they sipped their wine, a hovering waiter was there to replenish their glasses.

Lorraine took a last bite of food, a sip of wine, touched her lips delicately with the white napkin and laughingly told Micheline, "I'm as tight as a tick. Tell me again what it was I ate."

"*Yassa,*" Micheline laughed.

"Well, that *yassa* was simply marvelous! We have to come back here soon."

"I come here often, but I do not usually eat as much at lunch as we have done today," Micheline said, glancing at her own empty plate. "I will not be much good at work this afternoon. But I am only getting my dossier together for my trip to Saint Louis, and most of that is done."

"Why do you have to go there? Something to do with the embassy?" Lorraine asked.

"Yes. We have a pilot community health center that the Canadian government's aid department has contributed to, and I go up periodically to discuss its management."

"Ah, here is our dessert." Micheline rubbed her hands together expectantly as the waiter approached. They both had ordered fresh, sliced mango.

"Micheline, I don't see how I can eat another mouthful," Lorraine started to complain.

"Mango is not filling," Micheline said, cutting off a piece of the succulent yellow fruit.

"Urn, this is delicious. Try it, at least," she urged.

"Want some more wine?" she asked, when the waiter emptied the bottle into their glasses and turned it upside down in the wine cooler at their table.

"Why not? It was very good," Lorraine said, cutting a bite-sized piece of the fruit. "It's the first time I've tasted this wine. You say it's Moroccan?" She speared another morsel of fruit with her dessert fork.

"Yes. It comes from a small area near Marrakech called Boulaoune," Micheline replied, signaling the waiter to bring another bottle.

"Have you been to Morocco?" Lorraine wanted to know.

"Yes. Might as well visit as many places as possible while I am here. I never know where I am going to be posted next," Micheline said, glancing around as someone laughed loudly on the other side of the restaurant.

"To get back to our trip to Saint Louis," Micheline prompted, "we will stay at a small hotel there, but I will be spending the whole day at the health center."

The new wine arrived, but they found that their eyes had been bigger than their bellies, and after one more glass each, they could not finish the second bottle of wine. They ordered coffee, then asked for and paid the check.

For a moment, Lorraine's mind went back to Andrew. She tried to imagine him here and could not. When she thought about Momar, she felt an unsettling passion well up in her. She realized, with surprise, that she felt nothing when she thought about Andrew. She giggled, remembering how solid, dull and dry he was.

"Did you hear me? Hello?" Micheline waved her hands in front of Lorraine's eyes and laughed. "I said, how would you like to come to my beach house party this evening?"

Lorraine was beginning to feel languorous from the food and drink. She peered at her friend, waved her glass and said in a relaxed voice, "That would be lovely."

"Excuse me a minute, will you, Lorraine? I have to find the ladies room," Micheline said, rising.

Lost in thought, Lorraine's mind conjured up Momar making love to the African-Asian woman she had seen him with at the restaurant the other day. What do they say to each other? she wondered. Lorraine rotated her wine glass slowly. Her imagination drifted from Momar and the woman to Momar and herself. She closed her eyes as she remembered his hands caressing her face, her neck and going lower.

The sounds of laughter and friendly arguing drew her attention across the room-and there he was! Her temperature rose at the sight of him.

Micheline returned at the same moment. Lorraine set her coffee cup down as Micheline sat with a contented sigh. "Micheline, isn't that Mr. Diallo over at the bar?" Lorraine cried out in dismay, pointing toward the bar with faintly trembling fingers.

"Yes," Micheline answered, turning toward the commotion. "I will invite him to join us." She rose and headed for the bar before Lorraine could say a word.

In the days following his first meeting with the two members of the American film crew, Momar had fought with himself to forget Lorraine Barbette. Just thinking of her made him feel as if he had been content with false women. She definitely was a real, warm, and alive one. Momar remembered how her hair had felt in his hands. How her lithe body had felt against his. He knew he would go crazy if he kept this up.

Thus, he was relieved this morning when Badoye Koha had telephoned and asked if he would like to meet him after lunch at the bar of the Taranga Hotel's dining room. He agreed because it would give both men a chance to discuss the American film crew.

Momar was pleased with the choice of Badoye Koha and Aminata Baumé as the partners with whom he would be escorting the American film crew. Both were competent and serious. At the bar with Badoye, Momar reviewed the two American men. Sam Benson, the man who had introduced himself as the scheduling boss, was short, stout, and, it seemed to Momar, always spoke through clenched teeth. Momar wondered why the man was so tense.

The younger American man, Mark Whitman, struck Momar as being open, frank, and genuinely interested in Sénégal's cultural celebrations. Momar was about to question Badoye on the third member of the American film crew, the one who did not come to the meeting, when Micheline Martin approached him at the bar.

Lorraine felt infused with a feeling of warmth as her friend and Momar Diallo approached. The feeling started somewhere in her lower abdomen and spread slowly to her face.

"We meet again, Miss Barbette," Momar said softly in French, looking down at her. His ebony eyes held a roguish gleam.

Lorraine answered in French, a slight quiver in her voice, "Indeed we do, Monsieur Diallo. Would you care to join us?" she asked boldly, yet feeling flustered.

"Waiter, another wine glass, please," Micheline called.

Momar took a seat between the two women. When the waiter brought the glass, he held it up, leaned forward, his dark eyes meeting Lorraine's gray ones, and in a voice that made her tremble inside, said, "To our American visitor." Then he clicked his raised glass to her coffee cup. She was hardly aware of Micheline, who eyed them curiously from her side of the table.

Lorraine longed to have his arms around her, a feeling that had no doubt been intensified by the wine. He grinned, set his glass down on the table and touched her arm in a peculiar, searching way that sent currents of fire along her body.

"My goodness. Look at the time," Micheline exclaimed, staring at her wristwatch. "I will telephone you later, Lorraine, about the beach house party," she said, leaning across the table to peck her friend on both cheeks.

"Okay, Micheline," Lorraine replied.

"I'd best be returning to my office, too," Lorraine said tentatively. Remembering the run-in she'd had with Wilson Graves, Lorraine wished she could escape returning to the embassy—for this afternoon at least.

Suddenly, a light entered Momar's dark eyes. "Have you tried mint tea since you have been here?" he asked.

She found his gaze hypnotic.

"No." Lorraine whispered, a tremor in her voice. In any case, remembering the run-in she had with Graves made returning to her office distasteful. She waited breathlessly for Momar's next question.

"May I invite you to my apartment? I will make some tea for you. The best in town," he added. He held his breath waiting for her answer.

With a sense of astonishment, as though her soul had been unchained, she replied, "Why not?" She stood suddenly before she could come to her senses and change her mind.

Momar could not believe she had said yes! Every emotion in the galaxy surged through him and wild, primitive explosions went off inside him. He knew the sensations were really quite illogical.

Nevertheless, he was filled with tremendous anticipation, like a youngster on Tabaski Day, the day when Muslims hold the Feast of the Lamb.

"By all means then," Momar said with a sexy smile, "let us depart."

5

By the time they reached his apartment, Momar was somber and quiet. He unlocked the door and preceded Lorraine into his living room.

Lorraine found herself in a large, airy, all-white room with French doors that led to a balcony overlooking the bay between Dakar and Goree Island. An exquisite, colorful mural depicting the denizens of the Senegalese forest almost covered one wall. An etageré standing in a corner held African sculptures, masks and carvings. The low couch, covered in a sand-colored hand-woven cloth, took up the two other walls in front of which stood a square, lacquered ebony coffee table. The overall atmosphere, she realized, reflected his concept of a warm traditional setting. Suddenly she realized she was seeing yet another aspect of him: his domestic side. "Please sit here," he invited, still speaking French.

Instead of sitting, she drifted to the French doors.

"I will only be a moment," she said in French and disappeared through a doorway to her right. Funny, she thought, her French had never been better. She was astonished at how easily it came to her. Maybe it was the company, she decided.

From the balcony, she gazed across the busy bay, a colorful sight where freighters, cruise ships, and a variety of small pleasure craft clogged the waters. She stared at the ancient fort guarding Goree Island. She wondered if her ancestors had been among those who might have been held on the island during the period in its history when slaves had been brought there before being shipped to the Americas.

"This is for you to put on," Momar interrupted her thoughts.

"You startled me," she whispered, turning from the balcony rail.

"I'm sorry. I did not mean to. You may change into this through there." He held out an exquisitely embroidered Egyptian cotton djellaba. He indicated the half closed door he had just left. At her slightly skeptical expression, he added, "You will be more comfortable in this." She took the djellaba, and when their fingers met briefly, she felt a girlish, tingly feeling. Then she disappeared in the direction Momar had indicated.

When she returned to the living room he called from another room.

"Come into the kitchen. I am preparing that promised tea."

As she sat at the table, he bustled about, full of geniality and charm, again the sophisticated, urbane man.

Trying to study him dispassionately, a disturbing thought entered Lorraine's mind. She could not help wondering how many women he had done the same thing for. Had he brought the African-Asian woman here before her?

Momar deftly placed two tiny, green-colored glasses on the table and sat down. Then he lifted a small, long-spouted beaten silver teapot high into the air while trying to keep his eyes away from the beautiful woman sitting across from him.

She stared, fascinated, at the pale amber liquid that filled the glass half way to the top. He tasted it, set the teapot on the table, and returned the tea to the pot. Only then did she notice it was stuffed to the top with fresh mint leaves.

"I will gladly teach you to make tea like this and show you other customs of my country…I think it is important for us that you learn…and that we spend time together."

Lorraine tried to hide the secret joy she felt inside at his casual announcement. Although her initial American instinct was to say, "What about your African-Asian friend?" she did want to pursue her interest in this attractive diplomat. Lorraine couldn't deny that she had some problems to work out; her broken engagement to Andrew, for one. If she knew anything about her family, and his, she had not heard the end of that. She also knew there remained many things she had yet to understand about the man facing her, and not just about his country's culture. Somehow, she felt that he was holding back something from her, that he was not being completely open.

She decided to concentrate all her attention on the tea that Momar was turning into an elaborate ceremony_ She tried to study him coolly. He grinned more widely as her gray eyes met his ebony ones in a direct and, what she hoped, was a challenging way. Then she, too, smiled with delight as the full minty, sugary aroma of the tea reached her finely chiseled nostrils.

In a barely audible voice, she murmured, "Merci," as he clicked his glass to hers, a smoldering power in his gaze. Lorraine sipped the aromatic brew slowly, taking the glass in both hands, sighing with contentment. "Your tea is excellent, Momar," she said, her voice husky. "But I find it a bit sweet," she said honestly, hoping she didn't sound critical.

"We use almost as much sugar as water—this rock sugar," he replied, getting up from the table to show her a cylindrical-shaped block of sugar partly wrapped in coarse blue paper.

"I've never seen anything like that," she said, moving gracefully to his side to examine the sugar more closely.

He replaced the sugar on the sideboard near the sink and touched her lustrous hair with a caress that sent fire through her. He looked deep into her eyes, searching, feasting on her. She was more bewitched than ever, filled with anticipation of she knew not exactly what.

The heat spread through her as he put a hand on one of her breasts. She felt her nipple swiftly become as hard as a nut. It showed clearly through the thin djellaba. Slowly he began to rub and squeeze both her breasts, first one then the other. Next he moved his head down and used his tongue to stroke and tease her nipples with his tongue through the cloth.

Momar felt Lorraine's wanting radiating from her in waves. He knew there was a fierce, desperate urging within her.

Moving his hands down to the slits in either side of her djellaba, he reached to pull it up and over her head. Momar was surprised to see that she was not wearing a bra, and the beautiful swells of her perfect breasts made him gasp in delight. He moved to kiss the silky skin of her flat stomach, and they both became deeply buried in fiery emotion, the tea completely forgotten.

Lorraine became an insatiable sponge, with mysterious and mounting ferocity. When Momar spread her legs a little and moved her lacy white panties aside, the fire threatened to engulf her. He brought his stomach against hers, setting every fiber in their bodies trembling; the center of his power pulsated with a life of its own.

Lost to the magic of the moment, her hands went to his own djellaba and tugged. He helped her, pulling it off completely and spreading it on the floor.

Lorraine's gaze took in the gorgeous display of smooth ebony muscles before her. Momar's body was dark, powerful and strong. Her fingers eagerly explored his hard chest, then dropped to his hips, questing, both excited and appalled that she could let herself be seduced so easily. They both began to let their hands arouse each other. Their kisses became more eager, hungrier. Her swelling breasts conveyed a firm and welcoming invitation, rocking her whole being.

Then, with one smooth motion, he lowered her to the kitchen floor, onto his spread djellaba. He kissed her deeply, massaging her breasts, then he finally buried himself into her completely in a sweet, rapturous union. She gave a lingering moan of joy, lost completely in his every movement. The two became so intertwined, Lorraine never wanted to part. With mounting ferocity, the last delicious moment of shuddering came upon them simultaneously.

Afterward, the only sound came from a slowly dripping faucet. Neither wanted to break the mood, but eventually Lorraine felt uncomfortable. Easing herself up on one elbow, she slowly turned toward Momar, whose eyes were closed.

"You make good tea, Monsieur Diallo," she said, breaking the silence.

"And, you make good love, Mademoiselle Barbette." He returned the compliment with a sigh of contentment.

She sat up, her legs curled beneath her body, as she looked for her djellaba. "It was your mint tea that inspired me," she said mischievously, rising fluidly, pulling the djellaba over her head.

"What? Only my tea?" Momar challenged in mock astonishment.

"Could I have some more tea, sir?" During the whole time she had been with him they had been speaking French.

"More tea, or…"

"Or what?" Lorraine laughed, her gray eyes twinkling.

"More this." Momar rose and in one swoop, a pagan grin splitting his dark-skinned face, his black eyes full of merriment, he pinned her against the sink, his naked body hard against her.

"My God, how I want you!"

"I want you, too," she breathed as he began to move against her.

Her response made her dizzy.

His sealing kiss sang through her veins like an endless song. Each touch of his darting tongue sent sparks of arousal sweeping through her anew, igniting within. When he gazed down at her an eternity later, her naked form was flushed from the hotly explosive currents that had raced through her.

"Still want that tea?" he asked, peering at her.

She could only vaguely shake her head.

"Fine," he said and began to fondle a breast.

Their lovemaking this time was slower. It was a union of two souls that had wandered separate continents and had been waiting centuries to be reunited. It was a tranquil, calm feeling.

And afterward, when Momar held her, it was with no demands or expectations, only burning, life-giving love.

Lorraine felt content just to relax in his arms. She stretched with feline sensuality that once again stirred the smoldering embers of Momar's desire.

Much later he asked blandly, "Want to see my special bathtub?"

"What's so special about your bathtub?" she asked, trying to get her breath.

"You will see," he replied mysteriously.

She left him lying on his djellaba, propped on one elbow. As she found her own, she pulled it on for the third time! Then she padded to the bathroom and gasped at the sight before her. She had actually thought the bathtub in her hotel room was huge! "One, two," she corrected herself, "no, three people could swim comfortably in this bathtub." Now she understood why he called it "special." It really was special.

She let the faucet run until the tub was half full. Then she slid into the steamy water and splashed herself with his heady, scented aftershave lotion.

A half hour later they sat down again to tea, back in the kitchen. "I love your tea, your bathtub, and..." Lorraine stopped short. Was she falling in love with him, too? Gazing around the scene of their recent lovemaking, she carefully sipped the newly brewed mint tea. She noted the bamboo cupboard doors, the African wall hangings and the hand-painted tiles on all the counters. Anything to distract her from her blurting out something she might later regret. After all, there was still so much she needed to learn about this Momar Diallo.

Following her gaze, Momar supplied, "My hobby is cooking and I designed this kitchen myself, to suit my way of cooking."

"It's the first time I've seen wall hangings in a kitchen," she said, looking at one that depicted two chickens being chased by two men with heavy meat cleavers.

Looking at the same wall hanging, Momar told her, "That one comes from the Cameroons and reminds me of my favorite chicken recipe that you will have to allow me to prepare for you."

"What's it called?"

"Marfait," he replied.

Then the telephone rang.

"Bonjour," Momar had lifted the receiver on the first ring. "Aminata!" His voice took on a guarded tone as he began speaking in a language which Lorraine could not understand.

Who is Aminata? A cold chill seemed to penetrate Lorraine's soul. Suddenly, she felt very vulnerable. What had she gotten herself into? Silently, she changed back into her own clothes, then she made her decision.

Momar was so engrossed in his conversation that he did not notice when she slipped away.

6

"Don't take the telephone conversation too seriously, Lorraine," Micheline was saying urgently over the telephone the next day.

"But you didn't see him or hear his voice, Micheline. I feel like such a fool. I allowed myself to be so easily seduced," Lorraine wailed.

"Blame most of it on the wine," Micheline advised.

"I got back to my hotel after nine in the evening," Lorraine cried. "Some lunch date!"

"I got home at nine, too. So we are even," Micheline supplied, trying to lighten her friend's mood. "I stayed late at my office and had to postpone the house party." Then she added, "I have tickets to the Daniel Sorano Theatre for tonight. It is a gala. It will change your perspective."

"Well, it is Saturday, and I'll have all day to get myself in the mood," Lorraine conceded with not too much enthusiasm. Part of her hoped Momar would telephone and ask her out.

"Good. I will pick you up this evening at 7:30—nineteen hours and a half," she added, saying it the French-Canadian way. "You do not even have to drive," she added in her always-up voice.

Later, Lorraine knew she had to dress carefully to boost her sagging ego. She chose her new gold-flecked strapless gown with matching shawl and gold slippers and bag. She chose her most elaborate jewelry—gold hoops for her ears and a matching gold loop for her slim neck. The gown had caught her eye one day when she had seen it at Line's Boutique at the Hotel Teranga. The jewelry she had brought from home.

The high life song playing softly on the radio had helped lighten her mood by the time Micheline arrived. "Wow, Lorraine! Will that dress ever knock them out tonight."

"You don't look like a slob either in that skin-tight midnight blue jump suit," Lorraine rejoined, turning her friend around to admire her. Micheline gave a playful imitation of modeling her attire, and both young women cracked up. Then they were on their way. By the time they turned into the wide boulevard and came in sight of the theater's bright lights, Lorraine's spirits had lifted considerably.

The whole scene had a make-believe feeling, and Lorraine was impressed by the long line of limos. She watched them disgorge dignitaries, who in turn awaited the president's arrival.

Filled with tremendous anticipation, Lorraine joined Micheline and together they entered the central portico on the red plush carpet already filled with the Canadian diplomats. Lorraine was unable to suppress her excitement. A feeling of warm gratitude went out to her friend for the invitation.

Lorraine had the distinct feeling of not being in Africa at all, although the photographs lining the thickly carpeted hallway were all of local black stars with a well-known French star added here and there. The men and women, African and foreign, who were arriving could have been from Paris, New York, Rome or Montreal. The splashes of conversation were a mixture of languages.

Soon the president arrived, and they were hustled to their seats. They had hardly sat down when the curtain opened to reveal a military band in full dress uniform. The band began to play the Senegalese national anthem, and the audience rose to its feet. Then the lights dimmed, and before the play, a comedy, began, the good-natured audience clapped and laughed with lively animation. The air was filled with an electric, contagious excitement. Lorraine and Micheline reveled in it.

Lorraine was so enthralled at seeing *Un medicin malgre lui* played by an all-black cast that Micheline had to nudge her when the lights went up at intermission.

"The ambassador has invited us to join his party for drinks in the president's box," Micheline said when she had Lorraine's attention.

An hour and a half later, as they filed out of the theater, Micheline happily informed her friend, "We all usually go to Niani's after the theater, Lorraine."

"Why?" she asked dreamily, still under the spell of the play that had just ended, not to mention having met the Senegalese president!

"To cool down, if you like," Micheline laughed mischievously. Then, her blue eyes sparkling, she added, "Besides, tomorrow is Sunday. You can sleep in."

Lorraine had enjoyed herself so much that it had almost wiped the incidents of the day before from her mind…almost. In spite of herself, Lorraine had surreptitiously scanned the audience more than once, trying to see if Momar was present. She finally realized, with disappointment, that he probably was not in the theater.

Overlooking the edge of the bay between Dakar and Goree Island, Niani's was a one-story wooden structure encircled by a wide balcony. When she entered it, Lorraine was surprised to see that a sumptuous table had been prepared for the theater crowd.

After tasting most of the food, she chatted with several people she recognized from the Canadian Day reception at the Canadian Embassy. While Micheline drifted from group to group, Lorraine accepted a cool drink from one of the waiters, and with her plate of tasty morsels, she wandered outside.

It was then that she discovered the lighted swimming pool between the club and the bay. Looking up, she marveled at the trillion stars that gleamed as they had done for millennia. Lorraine followed their reflection in the pool. A meteor suddenly burned its way across the sky and the pool. Bedazzled by both the heavenly display and the profusion of pungent aromas in a nearby bouquet of exotic flowers she could not begin to identify, Lorraine closed her eyes and made a wish. She listened to the lilting strains of a kora drifting above the laughter inside.

Placing her plate and glass on the edge of the pool, she sat down beside them, unsnapping the straps of her gold slippers, then dipping her toes into the pool.

She hardly noticed when other people drifted out. None stayed for any length of time.

She overheard snatches of comments about the lights of Goree Island, about the ships waiting to dock in the harbor, and about the bright stars that were so close one could almost pluck them. The night seemed like a warm blanket caressing her slim shoulders.

Micheline had been right. She really was enjoying herself. Finishing her wine, she was debating whether or not to go back inside and get another glass when a tall man appeared out of the darkness.

"May I join you?" He squatted beside her without waiting for an answer.

She stared. It was Momar!

Reaching into his jacket pocket, he smoothly produced a bottle of wine and two long-stemmed glasses.

"May I?" He sprawled next to her, uncorked the wine and poured some into the glasses, deftly holding them both between his long fingers.

Lorraine was silent throughout the ritual and was careful to let nothing show on her face. It was her body that betrayed her.

"Your feet are wet," he observed, glancing at her wiggling toes in the pool. He smiled. "Do you like the sea?" he asked, munching on tidbits from her plate.

"I prefer pools," she replied, sipping her wine.

He continued to nibble from her plate, watching her. "Lorraine, why did you run off yesterday without saying goodbye?"

That didn't take long, she thought, stiffening a bit.

"Because I felt you wanted some privacy. You were speaking to another woman in a language I couldn't understand. What did you expect me to do?" Lorraine answered, setting her glass down.

"My, you jump to conclusions. I was speaking to a colleague. We always speak Ouloff. It is easier for both of us," he explained, his voice tense.

Lorraine really did not want to remember their afternoon of lovemaking and how it ended. She changed the subject. "Have you ever tried to juggle a plate of food, a napkin, and a glass of wine all at the same time?" she asked

He seemed to relax. "Yes, and I have hidden a bottle of wine, a bottle opener, and two wine glasses in my jacket."

They both laughed.

Lorraine was not sure anymore how she felt about him. He's so foreign, she thought to herself and she felt out of her element. She admitted to the primitive feelings he aroused in her, but she felt that by going to his apartment she had foolishly thrown herself at him.

She glanced at his profile in the full moon, which had just risen over the horizon, observing his finely-chiseled ebony face. "I saw Micheline inside. Did you come here with her?" he asked, rising and going to sit in a nearby beach chair.

"Yes. We went to the theater."

"Now that you have been here awhile, what do you think of what you have seen?"

Glad of the distance between them and the neutral subject, Lorraine answered truthfully. "I like your city, the people and the food…"

Since Momar still did not know what she did or why she was in Sénégal, he fished. "Have you ever thought about becoming a diplomat for your country?" He would never ask her directly again what she was doing here. It could be that her work was sensitive or highly confidential. He wanted her to trust him enough to tell him everything. Then he'd truly know how she felt.

She blushed. "Why, no. Why do you ask such a question?"

His voice sent quivers down her stomach. "I've never ever thought of becoming a diplomat because, from the earliest time I can remember, I've always wanted to, to…do other things." She knew she was hedging. But she felt she had already exposed too much to this man. Her film work here was her own business.

"Did you ever participate in debates on government in school in America?" he asked, a quizzical expression on his face.

"Why yes, and I was good at debating, but I never took it seriously," she said diffidently.

For reasons beyond her comprehension, he became enthusiastic at her answer. "I knew it!" he cried. "I bet you would make a fantastic diplomat for your country!"

His enthusiasm made her blood race. Perhaps he thinks everyone should be a diplomat, she reasoned, taking her feet from the pool. They dripped on her shoes, so she hurriedly placed them back into the warm water.

After a few moments, Momar joined her. He, too, took off his shoes and socks and rolled up his pant legs to dip his feet into the pool beside her. He poured more wine, and while they both had a feeling of intimacy, they avoided discussing their afternoon of lovemaking. They sipped the wine, each lost in their own private thoughts.

To break the silence, she asked about his work and whether he would be sent abroad in the near future. He was noncommittal. When he stretched out beside the pool, his feet still in the water, she felt the vibrations from his body to hers. He lay prone. Then he turned to face her, their eyes locked, she felt hypnotized.

Finally he asked, lazily, "Are you thinking about home?"

She wondered why he would ask such a question. Reluctantly, she replied. "No. Not really. But I was thinking about a friend back home."

"Oh? What kind of friend?" He watched her closely as she answered.

"My old boyfriend," she replied in a reticent way. "Why do you ask?"

He lowered his voice to answer because someone had wandered outside. "Micheline said something about your having broken off with a childhood beau just before you came here," he answered. He fell quiet again.

In the silence, Lorraine began again to compare the two men.

After a few moments reflection, he apologized. "It is none of my business to pry into your personal life. Excuse me." He got up. So did she.

"You don't have to apologize." She touched his hands and started a heat wave. He dropped back into the chair, brushing her hands with his lips, his eyes suddenly fireballs. So were hers.

"I want you," he whispered.

Surprised, she remembered it was her signals at lunch a few days before that had caused them to make love at his apartment. The familiar urgency began again in her body.

Pulling away to put on her slippers, she tried to evaluate the meaning of their lovemaking, of his words, and to understand the reason they were so drawn to each other. "I don't know what to think, Momar."

"It was my invitation. I love you," he answered, vehemently.

"But I shouldn't have accepted," she rebutted, tingling.

He had returned to the chair and straightened in it, his eyes serious. Then he said gravely, "Lorraine, I want you to know something. I have had other women before, as you must know. They were only physical attractions. What you and I have is much more. It is as if you and I are predisposed to mix the blood of our ancestors."

"You couldn't be serious about that." Lorraine laughed, her shoes now on her feet.

In a singularly mild, firm voice, he replied, "I am serious. I want to be with you."

"I just don't know…" she began, but he suddenly changed the subject before she had a chance to refuse him.

"What was the play you saw tonight?"

Lorraine remembered Momar was a diplomat, accustomed to avoiding confrontations and smoothly maneuvering things his way. In fact, it was his job! Relieved for the change of course, she replied, "Moliere's comedy, *Un medicin malgre lui.*"

"I know it," he said quietly. But he was not about to give up on their relationship. "We must start fresh, Lorraine. A quiet dinner someplace?"

He stood up and drew her to him.

"You never give up do you?" she asked weakly.

Glowing, he answered softly, "No." He bent and kissed her, brushing his lips across hers. The burning memory of their lovemaking immediately flooded her being.

She tried to pull away but he gently restrained her. He lowered his head again, and she felt herself melting. When he allowed her to come up for air again, she pulled away and ran to the other side of the pool. He ran after her, then remembered he was barefoot. He stopped to pull on his socks and shoes before he pursued her. She felt a bit foolish, and they both were laughing when Micheline appeared on the opposite side of the pool.

"Shall we go, Lorraine? Oh, hello there, Momar."

"I will take her home, Micheline," he volunteered, still laughing.

Micheline knew when not to argue. She and Lorraine embraced and she was gone.

7

Some days later, after a brief trip to Saint Louis with Micheline, Lorraine was back in the sweet embrace of her handsome African lover. It was Saturday morning, and Lorraine lazily watched Momar dress to go home. They had shared a night of wonders. She'd never known anyone who made love the way he did.

Mid-August was still hot and muggy in Dakar. Although her room at the hotel was air-conditioned, Lorraine lay naked on top of the sheets. She moved sensually and noticed with pleasure that Momar's dark eyes glittered with instant desire.

He glided, in his panther-like way, to the bed and began caressing her hard nipples. She undid his pants and pulled them down to his ankles. She had never before let her hair down so much as she had with Momar.

He was sweating. "You are insatiable," he told her. "Me too. I cannot stop making love with you. I will be frank. Since my wife died, I do not usually see the same woman more than twice. But I cannot get enough of you." He told her more than once that he thought she was special. Their ensuing lovemaking was intoxicating, passionate where her sensual appetite exceeded his. Their heat slowly faded.

In the lull, Momar stirred. "Lorraine, I have to go to Zaire this evening."

"When will you be back?"

"I do not know. A few days, a week. I must settle Mai's estate," he replied.

"Momar, there is something you haven't told me about your wife."

"I know," Momar told her, his voice husky. He rolled onto his back, his hands supporting his head, staring at the ceiling. "I have had some very strong feelings of guilt about her death. Although ours was an arranged marriage, we were good friends."

He turned his head, his dark eyes searching her gray ones.

"You have no idea how many times I have told myself that if I had not allowed Mai to return to her village that night she would be alive now." Turning to face Lorraine, he went on, "Mind you, I hate to think of what my situation would be since I met you. I could not have remained with her. And yet, it would have been very difficult to obtain a divorce. Mai was a very rich, well-educated woman from a very powerful family, one that does not believe in divorce. We were never in love with each other. We met when we were both students in Paris. There were not many Africans in Paris then. When her family found that she and I were living together, they insisted we marry. They did not realize we were merely sharing an apartment because there was a housing shortage in Paris. So we married. Mai tried to be a good wife."

"Were you ever in love before we met?" Lorraine asked, pulling the sheet up to her neck.

Momar didn't answer right away. He closed his eyes, looking into his past, trying to remember if what he had felt for Therese, a Catholic Senegalese girl he had known at the lycée, had been love. She had been the prettiest and the most popular girl at the school. She had laughed in his face the day he had rashly declared his love for her after she had allowed him to carry her books.

At the time, he had been heartbroken. He had become bitter, sullen and silent, drowning his sorrow in books.

Funny now, he could not remember what Therese even looked like. He opened his eyes to gaze upon the warm, beautiful woman next to him. "No," he replied sincerely.

Lorraine nodded, understanding that he was being truthful with her. She appreciated his words. He was revealing his inner feelings, and inadvertently explaining one of the reasons he found her so different from the other women he had known. She sensed his ambivalence about a long-term involvement, but then again, she would not be in Sénégal long, so how could there be any permanence to their relationship? Momar knew she would finish her work, then return to New York. He was offering her his friendship while she was in Dakar, and when she left, Lorraine knew they could do nothing but say "bye bye" and part with the memories of their mutual foreign affair.

Into the silence Lorraine mused, "When I think back, I wonder how I could have allowed Andrew and my family to talk me into getting engaged to him. But I was used to my family making major decisions for me. You might say I was brought up in the style of a bygone era. My family believes in honoring the family, honoring the traditions…they were strict with me. You know, Andrew is the only other man I have been with, and we were engaged…"

Her voice trailed off. She hoped he would not misunderstand and think she was hinting for a proposal.

"Come with me to Zaire," he cried suddenly.

"I am here to work, Momar. I can't just go off like that."

"You never did tell me what exactly your work here is…"

"No. I never did, did I?" she teased, glad he had not misunderstood her statement about the engagement.

Momar recognized an evasive tactic when he heard it, and he decided not to press the point for the time being. In fact, it had become a kind of game between them now.

Lorraine scrambled from the bed, her jet black hair cascading over her shoulders, her only covering. When she returned to the room, clutching a terry cloth robe, Momar brushed her lips with his and was gone.

For some time after Momar left, she felt a warm glow. Her mind kept returning to last night and this morning. She would never forget a single detail of it. Her thoughts filtered back to the day she had first seen him on the plane. Her musings were interrupted by the shrill ringing of the telephone.

She impatiently pulled her thoughts together and lifted the receiver.

"Lorraine Barbette, *bonjour.*" *Boy, am I ever becoming Frenchified*, she mused.

"Lorraine, Sam." Immediately her mind was filled with sour thoughts. Before she could react, Sam continued, "The ministry has okayed our shooting schedule. We got work today and tomorrow and the days after."

"Today? How soon?" she asked, annoyed that she didn't get more notice.

"Mark and I will pick you up in an hour. You have your copy of our proposed scheduled shoots, don't you?"

"Yes. I brought them with me to study," she said dully.

"Okay, shake a leg then. You know the saying, 'Make hay while the sun is shining'." He laughed at his own wit and abruptly hung up. Lorraine dressed as quickly as she could, picked up her briefcase and purse and was waiting in the reception room when she spotted, turning into the hotel parking lot, the familiar minivan which the ministry lent the crew for work.

After greeting one another and shaking hands with their guide and chauffeur, Diop, Lorraine climbed into the front seat. "Any preferences of first places to shoot?" she asked.

Mark replied, "You're the director and producer on this, Lorraine, so whatever you say goes."

Sam spoke up then. "Yes. Except when it has to do with the scheduling."

Mark added, territorially, "Or the filming. So, the ball's in your court."

"Okay, then, let's begin behind the hotel at the lagoon, where there is water skiing. It's just down the road. Then, we'll do the island beyond."

Diop put the van in gear, and in a few moments they were piling out at N'Gor Village, Sam and Lorraine with their clipboards.

In addition to the dozens of water skiers in the lagoon, there were the Lebou fishermen, who have inhabited the village since primitive times. Lorraine asked permission to film the graceful Senegalese women who glided along the beach, balancing on their heads receptacles containing pineapples, bananas, oranges, and candies for sale. They also sold coconut oil, which they swore was far more efficient in helping the tanning process than any commercial product. There were droves of small children selling trinkets and men selling masks and fake jewelry.

Lorraine and Mark were in their glory. "We have to get all of this, Mark. Use your wide-angle telephoto lens for the water skiers; that way we'll get the island and the bay, too," she directed while Mark struggled with the cameras. Hardly allowing him to begin work, she went on, "Use the 200 ASA color film for the beach scenes."

After a short time, Sam ambled up to where they were working. He tapped his huge wristwatch before stating, "I hate to break this up, but we're due to film a few of the hotel swimming pools before we film the markets, and we want to get as much work done today as possible before the rains come again."

Consulting her own slim wrist for her watch, Lorraine tapped Mark on the shoulder. "Let's wrap it up here then, Mark." Mark reluctantly stopped filming the crowd of grinning and jostling children who were holding up their wares.

Diop held out his hand to help with the cameras. "Thanks, Diop." Mark was grateful. Diop steered them through the children and back to the van.

If they were awed by the magnificence of the hotel swimming pools, the scene surrounding the Sandaga Market sent them into raptures of exclamations.

Mark could not contain his joy. "Wooee! This is a cameraman's dream! Just look at the thousands of yards of cloth of every description. And look at that building. What would you say that is, Lorraine?"

"It looks, let's see, like dark ochre, built in a vague Sudanese style…"

"You mean you really have an idea of what style it is?" Sam asked, incredulous at the crowds surrounding them.

"Sure. It's the Sandaga Market," Lorraine answered, grinning as if that explained everything.

They entered the market. It resembled an Asian cara-vansary and was filled with a dense and variegated crowd. The customers had come to haggle over the prices of vegetables, fruits, spices, powders, potions, live chickens and meat. The wares spilled outside the market, all displayed on planks of wood. On the street the cloth displays gave way to jewelry, and alongside the cloth merchants were male sewers furiously peddling away at their vintage Singer sewing machines.

Lorraine could hardly keep up with Mark as he filmed, using first a sixteen-millimeter camera then switching to a thirty-three millimeter. Diop walked alongside, explaining the activities while Lorraine made notes as fast as she could.

Sam trudged along, constantly glancing at his watch.

For contrast, Sam scheduled the other market, the European market, Kermel. When they arrived there, they could see the pace was less frenetic and the wares were displayed more like in an American supermarket. Even so, Mark could not resist filming the smiling Kermel flower sellers, who displayed bouquets of flowers perched on their heads as well as clutched in both hands. Their long dresses were often as colorful as the flowers they sold.

Flopping down at an outdoor cafe opposite the Kermel Market and idly noticing women entering and leaving their chauffeur-driven cars, Lorraine inquired, "Where to now, Sam?"

"Let's see if our schedules match first," he said, pulling a wire-backed chair up to the table.

Diop and Mark drew up chairs, too.

"My schedule says Sembedioune," Mark said, his thumb moving along a page on his note pad.

"Mine, too," Lorraine sighed. "I was just hoping Sam had changed his mind. I would rather a downpour than this overwhelming heat." She wiped her face with a tissue, balled it up and dropped on the table.

They all ordered citron presses, freshly squeezed lemon juice with plenty of ice, and drank thirstily. They silently watched the bustling market scene. Sam paid for their drinks, and they all left without further conversation as though the effort of conversation was too much in the heat. At the artisans' village of Sembedioune, Mark did close-ups of the weavers, the beautifully displayed filigree of gold and silver, and of the leatherworkers. The leatherworkers turned the tables on them by giving all of them autographed photographs of themselves working.

"Who will believe such nobleness?" Lorraine remarked to no one in particular, carefully putting away her autographed photograph.

Mark was just finishing filming a display of masks when Diop pointed to an armada of fishing boats arriving at the beach beside the village.

"We can't miss that!" Mark yelled to Sam and Lorraine, while he and Diop loped toward the beach.

When Sam and Lorraine caught up, Mark had already waded into the churning surf to catch the right angle of the colorfully decorated boats loaded with fish of all descriptions.

Lorraine directed him to film the women and old men setting up stands to sell the still-flapping fish and lobsters, which were constantly attempting to escape. The beach quickly became crowded with housewives looking for bargains and haggling over the price of the fish and lobsters.

"Let's go, crew!" Sam waved to them from the safety of the curbside as Lorraine, Mark, and Diop mingled with the fishermen, sellers, scalers, housewives and small boys who carried the cleaned fish to waiting cars.

"Mark, be sure to catch the languages," Lorraine reminded, walking alongside the cameraman as he filmed. She recognized French, English, Spanish, Arabic, and Portuguese. There were also several African languages, and although she could not understand them, she could hear the differences among their forms.

In a few minutes the film crew and its equipment were reloaded into the van and heading toward the National Assembly building.

"Whew! I'm bushed," Lorraine said, hanging her hands out the van window where the outside air was unfortunately just as hot as it was inside. The air-conditioning had stopped working again. "Why do we have to do so much of this today?" she asked irritably.

"Because we go to Cayar tomorrow," Sam said, glancing at his watch again. Lorraine was glad that they were not allowed to film the National Assembly in session. They had to content themselves with filming its modern exterior. Sam fumed, "But they promised! I have the permit right here," he shouted at one point, waving the paper before the disinterested guard.

"Come on, Sam, before you get us into trouble," Mark insisted while Diop, embarrassed, tried to explain their situation to the bored guard to no avail.

They were all glum when they arrived at the ancient building that housed the Ifran Museum. But the elderly curator immediately enchanted them with his knowledge of the masks, statuettes, and royal memorabilia, collected from all over Africa. He allowed them to film whatever they wished.

Lorraine's head swam from the rich and varied exhibitions on display. But what fascinated Sam most was the cultural archives, which depicted animist customs of life from birth to death, the initiation rites, including circumcision, and the marriage and cultural rites. They all depicted scantly clad or naked human forms.

"Tell Mark to get good close-ups of that, Lorraine," Sam whispered more than once, finally sidling up to her to point out the last statuette, that of a very realistic, pregnant nude female form. Lorraine could have sworn the man was drooling. She sighed in exasperation.

"We'll do one more museum and then call it a day, fellows. I've had it," Lorraine said with a finality no one argued with after they had thanked the curator and taken their leave.

"I'll film the Catholic church on Monday, if that's all right with you, Lorraine," Mark said, drawing a line through something on his notepad. "And it if isn't raining," he added, laughing.

"Sure, Mark. Besides, it's near the embassy," she remarked. "You can film it any day, for that matter."

"Except when there are services," Diop added. They had forgotten that.

"Where is this Dynamic Museum, Diop?" Sam asked the chauffeur, who was maneuvering the van into traffic.

"It is after the village and the beach where we were earlier this afternoon."

"Why didn't we go there then?" Lorraine wanted to know, feeling irritable again.

"Because I had been promised that we could film the National Assembly in session. That's why!" Sam answered angrily. "How far is this place anyway?" he asked belligerently.

"Not far, not far," was all Diop would answer. Lorraine and Mark kept silent. Sam glared out the window. Diop broke the silence. "Mademoiselle Lorraine, maybe

Monsieur Mark would like to film the mosque as we drive by since we will not be allowed to go inside."

"That's a good idea." Lorraine was pleased he had broken the heavy silence, and eagerly began to direct.

"Drive around it slowly," she directed. Then, aiming her instructions at Mark, she said, "Use the zoom lens, Mark, and be as discreet as possible. People are already arriving for evening prayers." Men and boys, wearing long djellabas and carrying prayer rugs, were entering the holy place.

Mark whistled at the sixty-seven foot minaret and the elaborate Maghrebian-style mosque nestled in the center of a huge courtyard.

"The Moroccan government built it in 1967," Diop was proud to supply as he drove slowly around the edifice, giving Mark a chance to film it from all angles.

When they were on their way again, Mark mused, "You know something? This Dakar reminds me of the French Quarter in New Orleans."

One glance at the interior of the Dynamic Museum, and Sam returned to the minivan. It exhibited the art of contemporary Senegalese painters, a complete contrast to what they had seen at the Ifran Museum.

"Ten o'clock for Cayar tomorrow morning," Sam said, as Lorraine opened the door to leave the van.

She nodded and trudged wearily up the hotel steps. She ate a lonely dinner in her room while surveying the day's activities. Before she went to bed, she made a note of those places that she wanted to explore more fully.

At sunrise Lorraine was standing at the French doors, which opened onto the balcony of her room, wishing she could be on the lovely beach beyond the lagoon. Sam and Mark would be waiting for her soon. They would be in Cayar in a few hours. She knew Sam intended to keep a busy schedule even if it killed them all.

After this assignment, she mused silently, she hoped Sam would be gone from her life. She hoped she would never have to work with him again. His abrasive manner had begun to rankle her.

She looked tired, as though she had not slept all night. Her movements were stiff. She tried to lessen her heartache at missing Momar but was unsuccessful. She sighed and returned to her room to prepare for the arrival of her colleagues.

Micheline had not seen her friend for awhile and wondered not just about her relationship with Momar but about her work. The past few weeks they had only been able to get together rarely, and then only for a quick sandwich and without much conversation when they did. And also, Micheline had been spending a lot of time with her own boyfriend.

The sun was a little more established in the sky when Micheline called Lorraine.

Thinking it was Momar, Lorraine answered on the first ring.

"Micheline here." Lorraine tried not to sound disappointed. Although she was pleased to hear from her friend, she had hoped it was Momar telephoning from Zaire. Fighting the urge to cry, she forced a smile into her voice.

"What is your latest news, my dear? Got a minute?" asked Micheline first thing after saying hello.

"Sam and Mark will be here at ten. We're going to Cayar to film today. Can you beat that?" Lorraine asked. "We're behind schedule, and we didn't even get permission from the ministry until late Friday night. We worked all day yesterday, too," Lorraine confided wearily. "What about you?"

"Let us get together for lunch, and I will bring you up to date," Micheline said. After a few more polite banalities, they made a date and both rang off.

8

To set the proper mood for Cayar, Diop took them to the communal station where the bush taxis and car rapides were being loaded for the destinations outside Dakar.

"Now that's the way to travel," Sam laughed as Mark filmed. The vehicles were decorated with thousands of inscriptions in every imaginable color. Diop explained as Mark filmed, "The inscriptions make fun of the various stations along their routes."

Lorraine told Mark, "Make sure you get those, and the running boards. Those are the widest running boards I have ever seen!" she exclaimed.

"Say, Diop," Mark stopped filming for a moment, to watch a car rapidly being loaded. "How many people can one of those things hold?"

Diop laughed before answering, "They are supposed to hold from fourteen to twenty-four people, but they usually carry many more."

"I can see that," Lorraine added, laughing too. "I can count almost fifty people already in that one," she said, pointing to a car rapide where people were stuffed inside like cord wood. They were holding on, precariously, to the roof while sticking their feet inside the vehicle.

"Do they have schedules?" Mark asked, filming the car rapide Lorraine had indicated.

"They leave when they are full," Diop laughed again.

"Boy! Look at all those packages: baskets loaded to the brim, chickens, goats, and sheep all tied to the roof of that one!" Lorraine was so fascinated, she almost forgot to tell Mark to film it before it left.

"What a way to travel!" Sam repeated. "But it's time to go. Let's get going."

After a few minutes on the paved street, they turned off onto a gravel road where they bumped along under over-hanging, heavily-scented, flowering trees. Shortly they came to a small nondescript building which had KEUR MOUSSA written above the door: MOUSSA'S HOUSE. The film crew knew this couldn't be Cayar so soon but before anyone had a chance to question him, Diop turned off the motor and turned to face them, a huge grin splitting his dark face.

"Surprise! This is a Benedictine monastery, and I thought you would like to see their mass. It must be different, you will see," he promised. To their slightly inquisitive faces, he urged, "Come on. But leave the cameras here." Mark, who was reaching for one, withdrew his hand.

In a moment they saw what Diop had meant. Mass was being celebrated with koras, balafons and tambourines, making an unusual sound to say the least. "Well, I'll be darned," Lorraine whispered to Mark. "I could swear I was in a holiness church back home in Mississippi. There is one exception, though."

"What's that?" Mark whispered back.

"Those white priests and those black novices," she grinned.

"I wish I had my cameras," Mark whispered again. "Just look at those red frescoes and the explosion of flowers and birds."

Later, Lorraine was disappointed to find that Cayar was only a small thatch-roofed village of huts and barracks made of planks. It had one street and it led only to the beach.

But the extraordinary spectacle of the famous return of the dugout canoes more than made up for her disappointment.

Mark went wild filming the elongated forms of the dugout canoes, which were painted in lively colors and dangerously overloaded with the day's catch. He filmed the sou'westers and the woolen caps worn by the fisherman. He filmed the triangular sails of certain skiffs and marveled at the expertise with which they took the waves, and at the mountain of fish of all sizes.

He rushed into the water to film the fish flapping on the sand, the women's greetings and the children who came to take charge of the sea's booty.

When Mark had finished filming the spectacle there, another one awaited them. Farther along the beach, thousands of fish were slit and laid out on high platforms to dry in the sun.

Lorraine met Micheline a few days later at a lunch that had taken barely a few minutes longer than the time it took to grab a sandwich. After the usual cheek pecking and greeting, Lorraine had a chance to observe her friend. She remarked with a worried frown, "Micheline, you've lost weight. Are you working too hard? Are you all right?"

"Everything is fine. No, I am not working too hard. And how is your own work doing?"

"Don't try to turn the subject, Micheline Martin. You look tired. And you haven't laughed a single time since we've been sitting here. That's not like you. If it's that boyfriend of yours that's causing you trouble, stop seeing him. Advice from Sister Lorraine." Lorraine hoped her teasing tone would cheer her friend.

She was pleased to see Micheline laugh at her feeble attempts at humor. They made a date to explore the beaches behind Lorraine's hotel and said goodbye.

The following Saturday, Lorraine had time to reflect on her so-called advice to Micheline as she swam in the bay off N'Gor Island. She stared at the distant ships. She floated on her back and bobbed on the waves as the French Concorde took off from Yoff Airport nearby.

"Lorraine, come ashore," Micheline called from the island. She had put on a colorful skirt and was applying the local coconut oil to her torso and arms.

"You keep that up, Micheline, and you'll be as brown as I am," Lorraine laughed, coming from the water like a sea nymph. The water cascaded off her sleek, fashion-model frame.

"I'm famished."

"Fine. This roast chicken will taste good," Micheline said, laughing and doing a little gypsy dance in the hot sand.

The two had the small island to themselves this Saturday afternoon. Their picnic had been prepared by the N'Gor Hotel kitchen staff. Lorraine plopped down on the huge towel next to Micheline, who had laid out the real silver, glassware and china with linen napkins the hotel staff had generously supplied.

Their lunch consisted of the chicken, a green salad, fresh fruits and chilled white wine. "Can you go with me again to Saint Louis, Lorraine? You never gave me an answer, you know."

"Yes, I can. As a matter of fact, we're going to be filming there next week," she answered around a chicken leg.

The following Sunday afternoon, as they neared Saint Louis, Micheline told Lorraine about a small orphan boy who was a permanent patient at the center that the Canadian government sponsored. "The boy is a patient although he is not ill," she explained.

"How is that?" asked Lorraine.

"His father is an African-American. He pretended to be a doctor and, would you believe it, he actually pulled it off for a while before being found out!"

"What! You're kidding."

"I wish I was. He married a Senegalese girl who died in childbirth. That happens more times than it should."

Lorraine was staring at her friend now. "I have a lot to learn about this country," she said with a long sigh.

When they arrived at the center in St. Louis, Lorraine was surprised to see how tall the five-year-old boy was. He was as talkative as any parrot, she decided. After telling her his name was Mamadou, the boy showed her around the children's clinic of the community health center as if it belonged to him. Micheline had left her in his care while she attended to business.

An hour had gone by when the Canadian woman returned. From the look on the boy's face, it was apparent that the young Mamadou had made a new friend. Lorraine's first words confirmed it. "I was telling Mamadou about America," she said. "He wants to go there, to see his father's country."

"You will get to North America one day soon, Mamadou," Micheline assured him. He beamed. Lorraine guessed that she was the first African-American the child had ever seen, except for his father.

Micheline sent the boy outside to play with the day care children. He went obediently, but only after solemnly shaking their hands.

"You certainly have a way with the boy," Micheline commented when Mamadou had left the room. "I have never seen Mamadou take to a stranger so quickly. What is your secret? It took me weeks to win his trust."

"Can he leave the center?" Lorraine asked.

"Certainly. He comes to Dakar with me often," she said to Lorraine.

"Why?" Lorraine asked before thinking.

"Because I am adopting him." Micheline replied.

That threw Lorraine for a loop. "How did he come to live here? And why didn't his mother's people adopt him?" She was bursting with questions. "Lorraine, believe me I tried. I wrote more than a hundred people in America when his father was imprisoned and his mother died. No one answered. Since then, we just kept him on here since this is where he was born. The boy has spunk. He is a wonderful child," Micheline finished, with a wistfulness Lorraine had never seen. "And the father doesn't want anything to do with him. Besides, practicing medicine without a license is a very serious offense in Sénégal, and it will be more than twenty-five years before he can leave prison."

"What about his mother's people?" Lorraine was shocked. Not that her friend would adopt an orphan, but that no family member wanted such an enchanting child.

"Lorraine, his mother's people come from the area near Ziguinchor, in Casamance. They are extremely poor. I went to see them. They live in a dirt floor hut. The grandfather asked if I could look after the boy. He said the family would be grateful. That is why I am adopting him."

At that moment, Lorraine realized that her friend was a rare human being. She was overcome. Such generosity was rare. Mamadou, she knew, would get to see not only the United States but Canada, too.

Later, Lorraine, being at loose ends, decided to drive across the bridge to visit the fish processing plant. She was going to suggest to Sam that they film it when he and Mark arrived the next day. Then, noticing a crowd heading for the beach, she parked Micheline's car and followed. The Saint Louis fishing boats were arriving. As in Dakar and Cayar, women, children, and old men quickly set up temporary stands while the fishermen's colorfully decorated boats rode the last waves. Once the boats were beached, the fishermen quickly jumped from them as the children crowded around.

The women and old men began haggling even before the boatmen unloaded their catches.

Carried away by the excitement, Lorraine found herself in the wet sand, looking into several boats and wishing that Mark could be present to film the scene, even though she knew it was a repetition of the other places.

She quickly drew back when a fisherman held a flapping fish close to her face. Then, on impulse, she asked, "How much?"

When he quoted a ridiculously low price, she laughed. "Why not? I'll take it." She had never bought a live fish before. She scrounged around in her purse for the money. As soon as she had paid the fisherman, a small boy took the fish and ran to one of the women who had set up her cleaning stand.

Lorraine knew she would have to pay the woman a few extra francs for cleaning the fish. She had bought the darned thing on impulse. While the woman cleaned it with people milling about, Lorraine recalled the day when she and Momar had bought two fat lobsters at the fish market on the beach in Dakar. Momar had cooked the lobsters at his place. They had eaten them as they drank chilled champagne. The memory left her feeling a mixture of emotions. How she missed Momar. His kisses, his teasing, his laughter...

"Your fish is ready, lady," the small boy said partly in French and partly in a local dialect, tugging at her arm.

"How much?" Lorraine asked in French of the woman who had cleaned the fish. When the woman replied, a wide grin split her beaming face because she realized that

Lorraine was not going to haggle over the price. She even carefully wrapped the fish in a piece of an old newspaper after she had pocketed the money.

The small boy accepted the fish for Lorraine and indicated that he would carry it to her car. They weaved their way through fish of all sorts and sizes, more people and stands.

When they arrived at the car, she shook the sand from each shoe before opening the car door. All the while her small escort was grinning up at her and fending off jealous friends who had followed them.

Lorraine gave the boy a handful of coins and told him to keep the fish, too. His expression of awe at the coins and at the fish made Lorraine's heart leap. She could see his friends crowding around him as she slowly drove toward the bridge to the hotel, the visit to the fish processing plant forgotten. The little boy had reminded her of Mamadou.

9

When he arrived in Zaire, Momar realized that settling Mai's estate was not going to be as cut and dried as he had hoped. His body was in Zaire but his mind was concentrated on the beautiful tan-skinned woman he had left behind in Dakar.

He thought he would go crazy with the endless details of who got what, how much and when. Giving away all their personal possessions to endless cousins, brothers and sisters was a very unpleasant chore. He did not want to keep anything that would remind him of his time with Mai.

"Let her rest in peace," he told his mother-in-law when she asked why he did not want to keep any of her daughter's personal things. What he had meant was that he would be more at peace with nothing to remind him of Mai.

It had been two days since Lorraine's trip to Saint Louis. The filming had gone well. They had sent all the film to Paris for processing and had edited it before continuing with the next session. She was exhausted. The last person she expected to see when she headed for her car in the embassy parking lot was Momar.

"I thought you were still in Zaire!" she cried when he called out to her.

"I have just returned," he said, taking her elbow, sending the familiar fire through her. "I will take you home."

"I have my own car," she protested. She sensed that his attitude had taken on a new intensity, as though his time away had been as much a personal wasteland as had hers.

"My chauffeur will drive it to your hotel," Momar said, steering her toward his car. Lorraine did not want to make a scene in front of her colleagues and the other office workers who were filing into the parking lot.

"Oh, all right," she agreed reluctantly.

They arrived at his car, and Momar said something in rapid Ouloff, one of the local African languages. His chauffeur got out of the car, opened the door for Lorraine, then held out his hand. "Oh. You want the keys to my car?" she realized and said in French. The chauffeur grinned and nodded. Momar slid behind the wheel of his late model, French-made car and brushed her lips lightly before starting the engine.

"You shouldn't have done that!" she cried.

"My place for tea?"

"No. Your tea is too sweet, and it leads to other things."

"Coffee then?" he asked, steering the sleek car away from the parking lot.

"Look, Momar. I don't want to be another notch on your buckle. You act as though you haven't heard a word I've just said. You don't own me."

"What does that mean?" he asked without taking his eyes off the road.

"It means that I'm just another woman in your life. You yourself told me that you never remained with a woman for long."

They were driving through heavy rush hour traffic which provided a remarkable human spectacle. Pedestrians streamed everywhere on their way home from work. From the huge parking lots, the brightly painted, overloaded car rapides lurched away with their passengers hanging on precariously.

Public buses and communal taxis vied with the traffic mass, their horns blaring. The spectacle, Lorraine decided, was one only Dakar could provide: a bustling city that had begun as a small fishing village.

I might as well concentrate on what I know about this place since Momar isn't listening, Lorraine thought to herself, crouching in her seat.

She knew that the local tribe, the Lebous, had given the Frenchman, Général Protêt, permission to settle when the Island of Goree became too small for his entourage. And thanks to Pinet-Laprade, the present city's construction began. Lorraine laughed to herself when she remembered an item from her research about Sénégal. Senegalese infants born in the four departments created by the French before independence were French by birth while those born elsewhere in the country were subjects. She laughed out loud, causing Momar to take his eyes off the road briefly to glance at her.

When the port was begun in 1910, Dakar replaced Saint Louis in population and exports, she recited silently by heart, quoting one of the reports she had read. Then, the governor-general of France had made Dakar his home since 1895.

Dakar's prestige soared when the French pilot, Mermoz, created the air mail link with Brazil.

Lorraine, watching the spectacle of today's traffic jam, realized that the people she was seeing reflected the populations lured to Dakar. In the short time she had been there, she recognized Lebous, Ouloffs, Toucouleurs, Peuls, Lebanese, Africans from other African countries, and there were always the French, Asians and other Europeans.

There were people of all colors. The Africans ranged in color from deep black to light bronze. She knew from her research for their films that when the French won the conquest for West Africa, Dakar replaced Saint Louis as the administrative headquarters for French West Africa as well. Administrators were brought in from all over French West Africa. As well, rural Senegalese left the countryside in droves, lured to the capital. Now, seated beside Momar, she suddenly blurted, "I don't want to become part of this!" Indicating the scene outside the car.

"I do not understand what you are talking about, *ma cherie.*"

"Can't you understand what I'm saying?" she cried, staring straight ahead. "And, I won't have coffee or tea at your apartment. You'll seduce me again, and then when your friends telephone you'll forget I'm there."

"What?"

"Everyone in Dakar seems to know who you are in bed with. Everything we do is public knowledge, Momar! I'm a private person!" She had been roundly teased by her colleagues about her affair with Momar. She had thought he would be more serious.

"Then let us go to a private place for coffee," was all he said to her illogical outburst. The man was unflappable.

He turned into the Corniche Road, not waiting for her to agree or disagree. "And, I don't care who knows about us," he declared in a moment, guiding the car into a space at the Lagon Restaurant, on Little Corniche Road.

"Well, I do," Lorraine cried, flouncing out of the car. He caught her by the arm, guiding her toward the open-air restaurant, which was built over a quay where chairs and tables lined each side. The wharf jutted out a hundred feet over the water, and bathers lazed at the far end, beside tall cool drinks.

They drank two tiny cups of heavy Turkish coffee. The constant roar of the waves breaking against the restaurant pilings became a soothing refrain.

When they returned to his car, night was fast approaching. He pressed his lips to hers. She felt like swooning, their near-spat forgotten. Because his kisses sent ripples down her spine, she was both excited and angry at herself for being so easily swayed.

When they returned to the center of town, the streets were deserted and dark. She remarked about it. Momar answered, mysteriously, "Dakar and Goree Island have many dark streets and many dark secrets."

After a long silence, when the only sound was the soft purr of the car's motor, Lorraine changed the subject by asking a question that had been haunting her for a long time.

"Momar, what causes families here to force cousins to marry?"

"It is an old custom to maintain all kinds of family traditions. Name and property elevate the family resources. All kinds of things…" His voice trailed off.

"I think it's an unfair commitment to ask of someone. But would you believe my own family did almost the same thing to me?"

"You have the same custom in America?" he asked, surprised.

"Not exactly. Some families that are close or powerful, or both, like to tie their power together through their children. But our social and cultural reasons are different from yours."

"What do you mean by that?"

"I mean that we can choose not to marry the person our families have chosen for us. The only repercussions we risk are that the families might get angry. Most times both the betrothed are happy to make their own rules because in my country we usually marry for love only."

"Here, it is more complicated," he said without further explanation. She had done her homework and had an idea of just how complicated it was. Family arranged marriages never broke up, she had read.

Although she had not noticed where he was driving to, she was not surprised to see they were in front of his apartment building. She watched as he left the car, then padded to her side to open the door for her. Once inside his apartment, he strode across the room and placed a kora concert on the player. She realized that, in spite of everything, she felt at home in his apartment. And yet, she was still a little on the defensive.

When she was with Momar, her mind overcame all reason. There was no room for anything else. She became almost wicked. Her thoughts ran amuck. She was lost in a mental fog.

"My cook has prepared dinner," Momar said from the dining room door. "We must not allow it to grow cold. Come." He held out his hands as he moved to where she was seated. She rose and moved to him as if pulled by a magnet.

Later, lying on his bed, Lorraine listened to the lilting strains of the kora drifting in from the living room. She looked up to see Momar entering the bedroom. His thin djellaba was transparent against the light behind him. His face was in shadow. He handed her a cognac as she scrunched up her pillow. They clinked glasses. She saw Momar's eyes searching hers in a peculiar way as he leaned forward and touched her trembling lips. She shivered. Lifting his free hand, he slipped his fingers under the shoulder straps of her slip, which she had left on before she lay on the bed. She lifted her arms to cover her breasts. He allowed his fingers to slide sensually over her bare arm, then fluttered to her neck. Then she felt their soft brushing against her cheek.

She reached out and clutched at his hand, closing hers over his. He leaned back, sipping the amber liquid contentedly, licking his lips serenely. She did the same.

Having finished his drink, Momar's gaze dropped from her eyes to her shoulders to her breasts. Slowly and seductively, his gaze slid downward as he eased the bed sheet, and her slip, downward. His gaze lazily appraised her, soft as a caress that sent a tingling in the pit of her stomach. A delicious shudder heated her entire body.

As he dropped down beside her, she moved toward him, compelled involuntarily by her own passion. The sweetly intoxicating musk of his body overwhelmed her. Her breasts tingled against the soft cotton of his djellaba. He pressed her closer. She buried her face against his throat. He whispered into her hair. Her soft curves molded into the contours of his lean body while his slim hands explored the curves of her back, making her body vibrate.

The caress of his lips on her mouth and along her body set her aflame. His lips continued to explore her soft, light brown flesh. Then, returning to her lips, the kiss was like the soldering heat that joins metal. It left her mouth burning with fire. Her senses reeled as if short-circuited.

Exploring her thighs and then moving up, his lips teased a taut, dusky nipple while his hands searched for her pleasure points.

He took her hands, encouraging them to explore beneath his djellaba.

She gasped when he finally lowered his body over hers, his djellaba cast away. It was flesh against flesh, man against woman, and she writhed beneath him. They were as one.

His expert touch sent her to such high levels of ecstasy that love flowed in her like warm honey. Together they had found the tempo that bound their bodies together and exploded together in a downpour of fiery sensations.

Afterward, she sighed and succumbed to the numbed sleep of the satisfied lover.

10

Lorraine awakened and stretched contentedly. Stunningly bright morning light swept the length of the room, leaving white streaks across the thick carpet of the bedroom floor. Last night's kora music was still playing from the living room.

"I was wondering when you would wake up," Momar said, a trace of laughter in his voice. He was lounging casually in the doorway, his eyes dancing.

Lorraine searched around for her slip, not answering. Having found it on the floor, she slid from the bed and slipped the garment over her head. Smoothing it along her body, she padded to the bathroom.

"Um, um. What's that delicious smell?" she asked.

"Fresh croissants and coffee. I was keeping everything hot until you awakened."

"I won't be long," she promised, disappearing into the bathroom. The remark Momar had made the previous night played over in her head as the warm water cascaded over her. "Dakar and Goree Island..." Momar had said. What exactly did he mean by dark secrets, Lorraine wondered as she showered in his huge bathroom. She, like almost all African-Americans, knew the history of Goree

Island since it concerned their ancestors. She was ashamed to admit that she had been too busy to visit it.

They were drinking their second cup of strong café au lait when Lorraine decisively put down her cup.

"Momar, could we visit Goree Island today?"

"Want to see where your ancestors stayed on their way to America, eh?"

Miffed at his levity toward something she considered very serious, she jumped up from the table so abruptly that she upset her chair.

"Yes. As a matter of fact I do," she replied.

Realizing how badly he had upset her, Momar stood up, too, and came around the table to her side. "I am sorry. That was callous of me. Of course I will take you there." He took her in his arms, holding her against his strong body until he felt her relax.

When they arrived at the quay on the Dakar side, both ferries, the *Blaise Diagne* and the *Saint Charles,* were there.

"Which ferry do you wish to take?" Momar asked after he had purchased their tickets.

"*The Blaise Diagne,*" she replied immediately. "It was named for one of your heroes, wasn't it?" Momar nodded his head. "I like that," Lorraine added, studying the sparkling white boat. They stood in the bow and watched the sleek white boat split the waves on the short ride.

Lorraine was glad that there were two policemen and Momar to help ward off the horde of small colorfully-dressed children who clamored to help travelers and tourists carry things. Even though she had nothing to carry, they crowded around her, insistent upon guiding her around the island.

Her mind went back to Saint Louis and Mamadou and the boy who had helped her with the fish. "I am her guide. Get lost," Momar said with severe authority, guiding her through the throng of suddenly silent, gaping children.

She forced herself back to the present. "I understand one can buy souvenirs made by the prisoners at the Portuguese Fortress," Lorraine said, turning in the direction of the island jail. "It's a good idea to have them make useful things, isn't it?"

"I suppose so," Momar answered absently.

She could tell it was not a subject that interested him. Trying to find a subject that would interest him, she stopped. "Momar, tell me about the island. We hear bits and pieces in the United States. You must know all sorts of details that we don't."

"We will buy your souvenirs, and then I will take you to the slave house," he said. The phrase eerily echoed in Lorraine's head. "…take you to the slave house." A small shudder went through her. A few minutes later, they were walking toward the main slave house.

"More than twenty million of our people saw their last glimpse of their homeland from this door where we are standing," Momar whispered, his voice deep and low.

Lorraine could not see his eyes because his back was to her. He was standing in the back door of the slave house, looking out to sea. "During the time of slavery, a ramp was attached to this door down which the slaves were taken to board the ships," he told her, still not looking around.

She realized suddenly that his earlier levity had been a cover-up. He had deep feelings about Goree Island, too. She was also very overcome with emotion, just being in the place. She was too overcome to move. Her eyes watered as she gazed out over the restless waves that washed against the back of the ochre-colored slave house. In her imagination, she could hear the slaves moaning and crying out as they were forced out that door, down the ramp and into the dinghies that took them to the ships moored a few hundred feet out in the churning waters. The curator had shown them the cells and demonstrated how the slaves had been chained to the walls.

When they stepped into the hard-packed dirt that was the front yard, Lorraine was trembling so hard that Momar, alarmed, asked if she was ill. She felt as though the spirit of one of their mutual ancestors had touched her. She could not tell Momar that. So she forcefully commanded herself to breath slowly, smile, act normally.

Later, in the curator's office, drinking mint tea after the tour, Momar told her in a sad voice, "The history of Goree Island is the history of slavery for both of us. The best of our people were taken away."

She saw that he was very affected at visiting the island. Although he could see it every day from his apartment, somehow, it was not the same. How traumatic it must be, she thought to herself, living daily with such a reminder. Maybe talking with her would help him to relax a bit.

To change his mood, she asked, "Who were the first people to use the island, Momar?" Her voice still was not clear.

Neither was his when he answered after a few seconds of reflection in a voice so quiet that she had to strain to hear him. "The Portuguese…in 1444. They were the first to start this, this slavery business here. Then the French followed. They were followed by the Dutch and the British. As a matter of fact, an English woman was the first white person to be buried here."

"That's interesting," Lorraine observed almost frostily. Sipping her tea, she wondered how many slaves were buried on the island.

"Some of the present schools, museums, and private houses were once castles of the slave owners." Once started, Momar seemed to be lost in the past as he continued. "But the only one preserved as it was when the Dutch built it in 1776 is the one we just visited," he added, referring to a house they had stopped at briefly before continuing to the slave house.

"How long were the slaves kept in those awful cells before being shipped away?"

His face clouding visibly, Momar replied, "Usually three to four months. Until ships arrived to take them away."

She wished she had not asked. Sympathetically, she added, placing a hand gently on his. "As a diplomat you must have to know all these answers, I would imagine, don't you?"

"Yes," he said, squeezing her hand, unaware of the effect his touch had on her. The sympathetic squeeze sent heat waves through her. "People ask about Goree Island and slavery everywhere I have been," he explained. "Even in the other African countries."

That surprised her.

"Want to hear more?" he asked, patting her hand.

She nodded, too concerned about controlling her temperature each time he touched her hand.

"Well, the Dutch were here between 1602 and 1779. Then, would you believe the British and French fought over the island while Napoleon was fighting elsewhere from 1779 to 1815? Then the Vienna Treaty gave Goree Island and Saint Louis to France."

"As if it was theirs to give!"

"Exactly."

"But the slave trade continued."

"Yes, until 1848."

Then Momar smiled for the first time and added, "You and I could be related, you know."

"I hope not. But how could that be?" Lorraine asked, mentally comparing her cafe au lait complexion and gray gaze with the ebony countenance of the man facing her with his jet black eyes.

"People from my tribe, the Ouloffs, were among those sold, as were the Sérere and Fulani."

"I know, and the Yorubas."

"The Yorubas were not Senegalese," he countered indignantly.

"I know that! But we know more about them at home. There were Mandingos, too, weren't there?" she said, returning to Sénégal, to mollify him. It worked.

"Yes. And the Mandingos were Senegalese. But they were rebellious, even though all the Africans were separated by tribes when brought to the island from the hinterlands to prevent escapes. The Mandingos, it seems, always managed to cause a lot of trouble." Momar laughed.

"I know. The Mandingos continued to make trouble for their slave owners after their arrival in the United States," Lorraine said. Then, her mouth curled distastefully at the thought that she was so close to the source of that part of the United States's participation in how she had become an American citizen.

Momar latched onto her statement about the Mandingos' behavior in the United States.

"They did?" he asked, surprised. "Yes. There was a famous Mandingo slave in the States whose feats have been kept alive in books and in the movies at home."

"Well, well. What do you say?" Momar was impressed.

After that revelation, they both retreated into their private thoughts and finished their tea in silence. Then they went to find the curator. They found him talking to a group of tourists. After they had thanked him and said their goodbyes, they returned to the dusty street. Before continuing, Momar asked, "Would you like to lunch here? There is an excellent restaurant on the other side of the island." Lorraine nodded. Anything to leave the slave house with its somber and sad history.

The sun was too hot for them to eat on the outside terrace of the restaurant that overlooked the bay between the island and Dakar. Although Lorraine would have enjoyed an unobstructed view of Dakar from the island, she appreciated the inside air-conditioning. Seated beside windows, they could at least look through the curtains at the city beyond.

When the waiter handed them menus, Lorraine began scanning it for something she recognized and burst out laughing. Surprised, Momar gave her a startled look.

"What is funny?"

"Did you read the menu?" she asked, still laughing.

"Yes, but I do not find anything funny," he replied, scanning his menu.

"What about this?" She read from her menu: " 'Pee and artichoke bottom.' It's the vegetable accompanying this shrimp dish." She laughed again and pointed to the attempt at the English translation. She would have read other translations, which were just as colorfully done, but the waiter arrived to take their orders.

"Could I order later?" she had to ask. She was still bursting with mirth.

Momar ordered the wine, and the waiter withdrew.

"Seriously, Momar. Tell me more about the island," Lorraine finally was able to say after having laughed her way through her menu. Momar forced a smile from time to time. The laugh was a good tonic for her after the slave house.

Later, as they ate the stuffed *Dem a la Saint Luisiene,* Momar decided it was time to change the subject of menu translations and continue with the history lesson.

"Here at the intersection of Rue de Bouffleurs and Des Dongeons," he said, spreading a small map on the table, "there was a woman, a Mother Jahonvev, who devoted all her life to abolishing slavery."

"No one molested her?" Lorraine was incredulous.

"No. The man that the Rue de Bouffleurs is named for, Chevalier de Bouffleurs, was governor of Goree Island at the time. It is said that he was too busy with his romances with the signarés of the island."

"Signarés? What does that mean? Who were they?"

"They were the light-complexioned girls."

Lorraine lifted a delicate eyebrow.

Momar continued, withdrawing the map. "Although they were slaves, too, they, ah…they had some privileges. Some even had their own slaves."

He did not have to spell it out. Lorraine understood. She added, dryly, "How interesting. The same things continued in the United States. Only the geography changed, it would seem."

Momar was ready to steer away from the subject, so he ventured. "Did you know that there is an island spirit?"

Lorraine shook her head.

"She was Madame Cumba Castel, spirit protector of the island and its inhabitants."

"I don't want to sound sarcastic, but she didn't seem to have protected the twenty million slaves shipped from here," Lorraine said, unable to keep the sarcasm from her voice.

"It is the legend," Momar said defensively. Miffed, he was silent as he paid the waiter. They left.

An hour later, as they waited on the quay for the ferry, Lorraine, curious about a building facing them, pointed a delicate finger and asked, "What's that old house over there, Momar? We didn't visit it."

"That is a police office now. That is why we did not visit it. No visitors allowed." He laughed, then went on to add, "But it is the oldest building on Goree Island. It was built in 1482."

"How did it get to be a police station, of all things?"

"It was originally built as a Portuguese church. Believe that. Then it was a warehouse. Then a forge. A bakery, a guardhouse, a fish market and a dispensary."

"Wow!" she gasped.

"It was taken over by the island police as their head-quarters after that." His last words were shouted over the noise of the horn blowing as the ferry approached.

11

"I think we should hire a second cameraman for the trip to Ziguinchor, Mark." Lorraine was standing near her desk, alone in her office with him. They had just finished going over the edited version of their latest batch of films. It had been a week since her trip to Goree Island.

Mark was leaning against the door frame, eyeing her slim shoulders, making her wish she had worn a dress with sleeves instead of one with the spaghetti straps. She knew she was between Mark and the sun. It was why his look was beginning to make her feel a bit nervous. She returned to her desk, sat down and picked up a pen which she twirled for a moment.

"Everybody else is out to lunch, Lorraine. Why don't we discuss this further while we go to eat?"

"Okay," she finally said.

"We haven't seen too much of you lately, Lorraine," Mark said, holding the outside door open for her. She did not answer. She wondered if he was trying to make sure she was on his side before they finished up their work and returned to the United States. She knew he was up for a promotion, and his performance in Africa could help make the difference. Her report, as well as Sam's, would count. They were the senior colleagues here.

"Heard you've been seeing a lot of that Mr. Diallo," Mark remarked, taking a sidelong glance at Lorraine as they strolled along the boulevard.

"I don't think that has anything to do with work, Mark," Lorraine answered tartly, never breaking her stride.

"Whoa! I'm not prying. Just trying to be friendly," Mark replied, holding his hands up defensively.

"Well…" Lorraine replied, hoping that was all it meant.

"Still friends?" Mark stopped and offered his hand.

"Oh, stop it, Mark! There is no reason to shake hands." She replied, a bit more sharply than was necessary. "As you wish." They resumed walking. Mark waved his hands in sublimation, and they continued their walk to the restaurant.

"Sam hasn't been around too much lately," Lorraine remarked at the restaurant. They had just given their orders to the waiter and he had withdrawn.

"He claims he's been working on a project at the Foreign Office," Mark said, playing with his wine glass.

Lorraine tensed at that bit of news. She wondered if Sam was trying to drum up official support for a private contract behind their backs, or if something else was going on which concerned only her.

"What is our position on the next assignment? Do we have any firm scheduled shoots for Ziguinchor?" Mark asked.

Lorraine brought him up to date on the shooting schedule they had. "As far as I know, that is," she concluded.

"You might be able to return home sooner than you expected," he volunteered.

"Why?" she asked, suddenly suspicious.

Mark just shrugged. "That's what Sam told me. I don't know any more than that." Lorraine wondered if Sam was using Mark to feel her out.

But nothing that Mark said afterwards during the lunch convinced her otherwise. She was almost paranoid by the time she decided toward the end of the day to telephone Sam at the Foreign Office. She needed to get to the bottom of his long absences.

"Sam must be up to something," she said to her typewriter. She could not get the suspicions out of her mind. She would insist that Sam tell her whose idea it was that she might be able to return home sooner than expected, after the Ziguinchor assignment.

When she got through to Sam, he said, in a placating tone, "Lorraine, you can take a week off in Paris on your way home. That is, if you don't want to go along on the Ziguinchor shoot."

"Thanks, but no thanks, Sam. And I'll meet you, Mark, and our Senegalese escort in Ziguinchor. I'm taking a week off since we have nothing until then." She added, "I'll be at Club Med at Cap Skirring."

He did not deserve the notice, but it was the correct thing for her to do in case anyone from the office or home needed to contact her. She replaced the telephone receiver. Numbly, she slumped into the chair, indecisive. "I just know there is something about the Ziguinchor shoot…Something that someone is not telling me." She let the sentence hang in the air.

Lorraine jerked off both sandals and threw them against the far wall as soon as she was in her hotel room. She stripped off her flowered linen dress and she felt calm enough to draw a bath.

"I need to stay in Sénégal! This is my assignment," she cried. She tried to telephone Momar. He was not home. She slammed down the phone in frustration. Even Micheline was out.

For the next two days she threw herself into her work, not certain about her immediate future. However, she tried to be positive. She was happy she did not see Sam. She trusted him less and less.

During the time Lorraine was immersed in work at the embassy, Momar sat in his office and mused. Lorraine had become so important to him during the short time he had known her that it scared him. She brought him a kind of happiness, a peace and contentment he had never before known. He felt that he could begin to take her to local affairs and that she would understand and fit in. She could experience the same pleasure he did being a part of his milieu.

In Dakar, social gatherings were major events, and people were on their best behavior, as though their lives depended on what was said and how it was said. Nowhere else in the world was palavering quite so important, and Momar wanted Lorraine to enjoy his enthusiasm for it. More often than not, though, they spent their time together at his apartment or at her hotel.

Therefore, a few days later Momar did his darndest to convince her to accept an invitation to a *mechoui* at Le Ramatou Restaurant. "It is near your hotel," he said when he telephoned her. "You do not even have far to go."

She agreed reluctantly.

When he arrived to pick her up, his first words, after brushing his lips lightly to hers were, "You look worried, *ma cherie.* What is wrong?"

"Oh, nothing important," she hedged.

He did not pursue the question, but regarded her with concern. He had never seen her in such a mood.

She had worked herself to a frazzle and felt irritable because of that, he decided.

She knew it was unfair to Momar, but her feeling of irritation remained after they arrived at the gathering. She felt out of place. She felt resentment at Momar, who was busy mingling, and he soon disappeared into the milling people in the fast-approaching dusk. She recalled that night falls rapidly in Africa. She found a chair. While she accepted the *akaras, merguezes* and other spicy hors d'oeuvres, she suddenly had a longing for balmy all-black Mound Bayou and the scent of honeysuckle and magnolia blossoms that lined and perfumed its quiet streets.

Other nights since she had been in Sénégal, she had felt good, even enjoyed herself. She knew she should be able to shake off her feeling of irritation and isolation, but she could not. She was still feeling so when Micheline found her.

"Hey, friend. You look as though you have lost your only friend," the Canadian woman laughed, her ever ebullient self. "Come on. I will introduce you to some new people." Lorraine allowed herself to be propelled through the crowd.

Somehow she managed to hide her real feelings from Micheline, who always seemed to have an abundance of energy and cheerfulness. Lorraine knew she should feel hopeful in the presence of her friend. She felt the opposite. She felt as though she were letting both Momar and Micheline down.

Momar took over when Micheline went to talk with some other people. He guided her to where a group of women were sitting in a semi-circle of chairs. They were being served the succulent roasted lamb and couscous. She was served in her turn. Momar disappeared again.

The colorfully-dressed Senegalese in their fine grand boubous, after initially making small talk with her, ignored her as they began to speak among themselves in Ouloff.

"Did you enjoy the *mechoui?*" Momar asked, turning on the ignition of his car. She felt as though a hundred years had passed.

"It was interesting, and the first time I have seen entire lambs roasting over open fires," she answered listlessly.

"You will get used to them," he told her, easing the car onto the main road. She was not sure what he meant by that. She felt that they were too different.

"We need to talk, Momar," she said, turning to look at him.

"All right. A cognac at my place?" he answered, not taking his eyes off the road.

When they arrived at his apartment, Lorraine sat on the edge of the couch while Momar prepared their drinks.

With a worried frown creasing his brows, he handed her a drink. Had he completely misjudged her *mechoui* crowd? Regarding her, he asked, "What is wrong, *ma cherie?*" Sitting down beside her, his regard had real concern now.

"What's wrong, you ask? Everything! You invite me to a *mechoui* and then abandon me in the company of women whose language I don't even know! That's what's wrong! I stuck out like a fly in a glass of milk at that *mechoui!*" she flared.

Oh no! he thought, but he decided to take the offensive. He had completely misjudged her.

"You are too American. That is your problem," Momar charged.

"What? You don't even know what Americans are like! How can you accuse me of being too American!" she cried, furious. "You're just being bull-headed and dishonest because you don't want to admit I'm right!"

He downed his drink and got another one without replying. *How can I make her understand why I thought she would enjoy my people and our ways?* he wondered, bewildered now.

"Admit it, Momar. We're too different," she cried angrily.

"How can you say such a thing?" he asked in a hurt tone.

"I feel more and more out of place here, the endless receptions and your *mechoui…*"

"Why did it take you so long to admit it?" he asked, his voice rising.

"Because, because I was trying to fit in," she cried. "If this is the way your life is always going to be, I don't like it." She thumped her drink onto the coffee table. "Besides, the colleagues I work with have been trying to convince me to return home." Even as angry as she was with him, she still had enough presence of mind not to tell him who these colleagues were nor what she was doing in Sénégal.

"Perhaps you should return home," he said, crushed at the idea of her leaving. "I thought you would enjoy yourself," was all he could muster in his defense.

She stood up abruptly, ready to leave.

"Please sit down, *cherie*. I will try to explain something to you."

Reluctantly, she resumed her seat.

"These *mechouis* are like our old time village councils, in a way. The elders palaver. The women palaver. The young people palaver."

"And just what exactly is a palaver?" she asked, her tone warming.

It was not the first time she had heard the word since she had been in Sénégal. Someone had even pointed out a huge baobab tree in a nearby village and told her it was the village's palaver tree.

"A palaver, in Sénégal, is a long parley, among the village elders, a talk. It usually takes place to work out some special problem. But at a *mechoui*, like tonight, it takes place between persons of different cultures. That is why I thought you would like it," he finished, sighing.

When he ventured a quick look at her, she had begun to sob quietly.

He pulled her to him gently, saying quietly, "Now, now, *ma cherie.*"

"I've always been a serious, private person, Momar. When we met, I expected to change, thought I could. But I can't." She hiccupped. "And, besides, I may have to go home sooner than I expected." She sobbed softly.

"Take off your jacket and blouse, *ma cherie,*" he urged softly. She did as he asked, noticing that he had never called her *ma cherie* so sweetly before.

He carefully placed her on her stomach on the couch. The cloth of the couch felt warm to her face and crossed arms. She closed her red eyes and began to relax. She felt him sit beside her. When she felt him undo her bra she drew a surprised breath at the tingle of his feather touch on her shoulder blades.

Slowly, rhythmically, he began to massage her muscles at the center of her back and the back of her neck.

She was not quite certain when she realized that his lips had replaced his hands, kissing her shoulders, the back of her neck, making her giddy with desire.

Momentarily leaving her back and neck, he slipped each hand beneath her shoulders and began to gently massage each breast. She squirmed and moaned.

"You do not like that?"

"Divine. Exquisite." She had never gone from feeling bad to feeling so good so fast. Momar repeated the gentle massaging, making her moan more. "Oh my goodness!" she moaned into the couch. But he seemed not to hear her. In addition to the gentle massaging, he again added feather kisses to her back and neck. He made her writhe and moan at the same time as his long, powerful hands and warm lips continued their ministrations.

Finally, when she thought she could stand not another caress or kiss, she felt him slip her skirt and panties down. She closed her eyes as he slowly turned her over.

This time their mating was wilder than anything they had done before.

Much later, she woke in his bed not remembering when or how she had gotten there.

12

The Saturday morning air was hot with moisture, like a steam bath, Lorraine reflected as she eased her rental car out from the hotel parking lot. She had plenty of time to meet Micheline for lunch. The thought played over and over in her mind, like a well-tuned kora. What would my parents, grandparents, Andrew and friends think of Momar if he went home with me? The idea gave her an inward smile. But a feeling of unease settled in when she realized that they probably would not understand his English.

Lorraine sighed. She had to think this through.

"I can go home early and admit defeat," she said angrily, slapping the steering wheel. "Or, I can stay here." But did she and Momar really have a future? And was Momar falling in love with her as powerfully as she had fallen for him?

A dark inner voice asked and reminded her that she was here to work. The thought struck her like an electric shock. Her personal life was beginning to interfere with her professional life. Her thoughts were beginning to terrify her.

She was the first to arrive at the restaurant. By the time her friend bounced in, Lorraine had allowed an awful pessimism to slowly take over her mind. She had realized that if she stayed in Dakar after her work was finished, it would be tantamount to deserting her hard-won career, her country, her family, her friends...everything she had known up to now. But then, Momar had not even offered her anything permanent. She was beginning to wonder if it was just a brief *affaire de coeur* they were having.

Micheline slid into the chair opposite Lorraine. Her blue eyes were serious for once, and her comment of, "My, my, Lorraine you look down today. Been doing some heavy thinking these days?" sounded more serious than usual for Micheline.

Lorraine, her face a surprised stare, did not answer.

Micheline continued, fluffing her table napkin.

"Has Momar said anything about his intentions recently, Lorraine?" Micheline asked bluntly.

"Not really, Micheline, and I might have to leave earlier than I expected."

Micheline's eyebrows rose in surprise, but she made no comment.

After they scanned the menus, Lorraine told her about her run-ins with Sam and her suspicions. "You would allow him to send you home!" Micheline bristled. Lorraine tried to explain her muddled mind and situation. "You told me when you arrived, Lorraine, that this assignment was what you had dreamed of. You broke off your engagement to accept it. You can not allow anyone or anything to interfere with it now. Your career is just taking off, for heaven's sake!" Micheline cried.

She went on. "Momar is a diplomat with a brilliant future. If you ask me, I am certain you could get a transfer here. Do it. You could even start your own film company where you would be your own boss."

Lorraine knew what Micheline said made sense. "Thank you, I needed your enthusiasm, Micheline." She felt like hugging her friend. Instead, she grinned and said, "Let's order. The poor waiter has been hovering for an hour."

Micheline's words remained in Lorraine's mind throughout lunch and after.

Over dessert Lorraine excused herself to telephone Momar.

"I am coming over," Momar insisted as soon as Lorraine told him where they were lunching.

"It's not necessary, Momar. I just telephoned to find out what you think about my returning to the States now."

"I was just leaving to go to my uncle's," he said, not answering her question, adding, "I want you to meet the uncle who brought me up." He had completely avoided her question.

She answered, "No." His invitation was far from what she had wanted to hear.

"You will not come to Uncle Barou's with me?" Momar was asking again.

The man never gives up, she thought. The way she felt she did not know why she was still trying to talk with him. But giving him the benefit of the doubt, and feeling that maybe she had answered too shortly, she told him, "Maybe I should just return to the States, Momar."

"Then I will go with you and meet your family." Momar surprised her with his statement.

"No. No. That won't be necessary," she said hastily.

"Why do you not want me to go to your home?" he asked in a hurt tone. "I have been to America only briefly, and then I met no Americans," he said tightly. "You know, Lorraine, you are really—how you say? Washy wishy. Make up your mind."

She had to laugh at that. So much for his trying to use slang, she thought. But she said, "Momar, you don't understand."

"Oh, no. I understand too well. You want to go home because you are afraid of breaking away from your old life," Momar accused fiercely.

Lorraine stared at the telephone as if it were Momar. She slammed the receiver down and burst into sobs. She hastily said a teary goodbye to a bewildered Micheline without explanation and drove to her hotel without seeing the road. She went to bed early, slept fitfully, and dreamed of Andrew, though it was more of a nightmare.

She woke up just before sun-up, depressed. One of her means of warding of depression was to exercise. She found an early morning radio station playing bouncy music, stripped off her night clothes and began doing an energetic aerobic dance routine. An hour later, after a hot bath, she was nearly her old self. She felt so well, in fact, that she drove into Dakar to see the city before it got too crowded.

She parked her rental car and began to walk down Boulevard de l' Independence. She passed the white presidential palace and smiled at the guards in their tall red hats. She stopped to ogle the peacocks in the palace garden, who put on a show for her by spreading their bright wings and tail feathers while strutting around.

This was far better than being on a film shoot or going to and from work at the embassy. This morning her time was her own, and she was determined to make the best of it.

She left the palace and turned down Boulevard de la Republique and circled back toward her car which she had parked at the Sandaga Market. She wanted to see it without her colleagues.

By the time she neared the market, it looked just as it had when they were filming. The streets had already become packed with people. "I shouldn't have spent so much time smiling at guards and ogling peacocks," Lorraine laughed to herself.

There were the open front stores, where salesmen were already crying their wares. There were the women dressed in their colorful grand boubuos carrying shopping baskets full of goods on their heads. Some of them, Lorraine sadly observed, were begging. Street urchins were running in and out of the crowds. Lorraine saw Mamadou in each child and remembered that she had forgot to ask Micheline how the adoption was going. She made a mental note to inquire the next time they talked.

Lorraine wound her way along, mentally comparing these people with the Senegalese she knew.

"I wonder if it's always been like this?" she asked herself.

The people I know are totally isolated from these people, she mused silently. *They have their chauffeured luxury cars, beautiful homes, private schools for their children...* before she could finish that idea she realized, with a shock, that in spite of the work she had been doing in Sénégal, she too, was isolated. But she had made up her mind several days ago that she would see more of the country, and without her film crew, Momar or Micheline.

She had told Sam that she was going to Cap Skirring, but she had not told him that she planned to drive herself. And she had not told Momar or Micheline at all. She wanted some time alone, to form her own ideas about what she saw and to absorb the feeling of the country as she saw fit.

Besides, she was finally going to get to meet the film crew's official Senegalese escort. The escort seemed to think the tribes around Ziguinchor would be less amicable to foreigners than the people in Dakar or Saint Louis. Thus, the crew would need the entire diplomatic escort for the first time since they arrived in Sénégal.

"Well, I guess they know their own people," she concluded. "I wonder if they have been following us around here without our knowing it?" She pondered that question for awhile but decided to let sleeping dogs lie. She concentrated on filling in the details of her trip while she mingled with the friendly crowd.

She tried to imagine herself as Momar's wife, shopping at the Sandaga Market. *But, if I was Momar's wife, I would shop at the Kermel Market, where the rich Senegalese and foreigners shop,* she corrected herself silently. She vowed that she would learn all she could about Sénégal, its history, its people, their customs, their languages…everything. She could not imagine any of the French wives or the Senegalese she had already met being comfortable in this mass of humanity.

A short distance from the market, she stepped into a *patisserie* and asked to use the telephone.

She woke Momar. "I just wanted to invite you to breakfast." She had wanted to have breakfast with him, although she had no intention of telling him about her planned trip. She apologized for waking him.

"What time is it?" he asked groggily.

"It's 8:30 in the morning," she chirped, feeling good.

"I cannot meet you. I have to fly off to Paris in two hours, Lorraine." His tone was not too kindly, she thought, her high spirits dampening.

Suddenly, she did not feel like chirping anymore. How could he do that to her with just a few words? Lord, she felt sick, humiliated that she had telephoned him again.

She hung up without saying goodbye. She paid the *patisserie* owner the twenty francs for the use of the telephone and numbly left, breakfast forgotten.

She no longer saw the throngs of people as she ran through the streets to where she had parked her car. "I have to go off to Paris!" she spat. All he had wanted with her was a dalliance. She was convinced of it now. It was over.

As soon as Momar hung up his telephone, he dialed his office to plead with the minister to find someone else to go to Paris. He felt sick, suddenly realizing he could lose Lorraine. "What must she think of me?" he asked miserably while waiting on the line for the minister's answer. "I will lie and say I am too sick to travel...I will..."

"Diallo, are you still there?"

"Yes, Mister Minister," Momar answered weakly.

"You are in luck. Someone else can go in your place."

Momar forgot to thank the minister and was out the door before his houseboy could heat water for his morning tea. He had no way of knowing that Lorraine had telephoned from downtown and he could not take the chance of her hanging up on him again. So he broke all speed records getting to her hotel. He almost grabbed the hotel clerk by the neck when the young man told him that Miss Barbette had left the hotel before seven o'clock that morning.

Forcing himself to think and act rationally, he asked more politely, "Did Miss Barbette say where she was going?"

"No sir," the clerk answered, eyeing him warily.

Momar decided that before making a fool of himself, he should return to the parking lot in order to decide what to do next.

In her car, returning to her hotel, Lorraine thanked her lucky stars that she had not made any rash moves. Her heart would heal. She tried to think of something to hurt him the way he had hurt her. "I'll let the air out of his car tires. I'll take the hand brake off it on a hill! Oh, no. That's so stupid," she railed. "But he always brings out the worst in me or drives me to make a fool of myself," she fumed, pressing dangerously hard on the car pedal.

"Before I met that man, I was—" Her words died in her throat.

She saw him before she saw his car. There was no way to escape. He was standing beside his car, next to the only available parking space. He opened her car door as soon as she came to a stop.

"Allow me to explain, Lorraine," he insisted, taking hold of her arm as she tried to escape.

"I don't want to hear a thing you have to say, Momar Diallo," she said angrily. Although his hand was burning a hole in her arm, she felt as friendly as a rattlesnake.

"Look. I sent someone else in my place to Paris. I need to talk to you."

"I'll listen to you when crows turn white!" she exclaimed, trying to wrench away from his grasp. Yet she was uncomfortably aware of his closeness, of the intensity of his dark eyes piercing hers, of the French aftershave lotion he used. He always had the power to disturb her.

A plane took off from Yoff airport, momentarily distracting them. She wondered stupidly if it was the one he would have been on had he left.

In spite of her anger, Lorraine's heart was beating like a muffled drum. She had learned from earlier experiences with him that arguing with him was like trying to extinguish an electric bulb by blowing on it. With a new feeling, like walking beside a wild animal, she allowed him to take her hands in his. His scent was more overpowering than ever.

"Lorraine, *ma cherie,* I want to explain to you that while I did not have to go to Paris, I must remain in Dakar, on call. We are not through, Lorraine. We must talk. But now I must go to my office, *ma cherie.* " He brushed her trembling lips. She gave a weary shrug, her face impassive as she watched him fold himself into his car.

She allowed her pride to conceal her inner turmoil, but a tumble of confused thoughts and feelings were assailing her. She was more shaken by his visit than she cared to admit.

Momar Diallo was a complex man. She needed time to reorient her feelings. Now, she was more determined than ever to get away for some time alone.

13

Momar drove around a long time after leaving Lorraine. He was forced to admit that there was something very special he had with her. Just looking at her was enough to twist his insides into knots.

It was easy to tell himself that he had come into his own as a diplomat and should be able to handle any situation, like the feeling of flying that possessed him where Lorraine was concerned. He should be able to have an affair with her and take it in stride.

Could he? Could he have an affair with Lorraine and let her go out of his life?

Momar knew that he had never given a woman even a measure of what he was capable of giving. He suddenly realized that with Lorraine, he wanted to give all. There would be no holding back with her, nor would he want there to be.

From a distance he heard the blast of a horn. A huge truck nearly on his bumper jerked him out of his trance. Alerted, he turned the steering wheel just in time to avoid drifting into the median lane and colliding with an oncoming car.

When he arrived at his office he found a note propped against the telephone on his desk. The Minister of Foreign Affairs, his boss, wanted to see him.

"Now what?" Momar snarled. Balling the message into a wad, he threw it into the wastepaper basket. Moments later he received his orders.

"Diallo, the government has promised the Tanda tribe that their privacy will have the full protection of the law this time."

Momar did not answer immediately, and when he did, he asked, "Has it been five years already since their last initiation ceremonies, Your Honor?"

"Yes, it has. And you would be surprised to know what foreign film companies are offering and have been doing in order to film the ceremonies. Make sure you are present in Ziguinchor during those ceremonies. I want you to be my liaison officer in this matter. You will report both to the Foreign Office and the Ministry of Information, since you are already part of that escort team for that American film crew."

Momar decided that this did not sound too good. Although being liaison officer for the Foreign Office was a step up, he still had to contend with that American film crew. Momar studied the minister's expression. It was harried, apologetic. The minister knew more than he was saying. Something was up.

Momar dropped into the vacant chair in front of the minister's desk. "What is it? Has the office any suspicions?" Momar finally asked outright. The minister walked around his desk and, before sitting, pushed a beige folder toward Momar.

"Here is the schedule for your American film crew. But their scheduling boss, Sam whatever his name, has been working here for over a month now. I have every suspicion that he has been attempting to gain the confidence of our staff. We have reason to believe that he is up to something that is not on their schedule."

Momar let out a whoosh. He was grateful for the minister's succinct and honest reply. "We have had a meeting with two of their crew," Momar told the minister. "However, I have not yet met the third crew member."

"You will meet everyone in Ziguinchor," the minister assured him. "The Minister of Information has already sent along the other two members of your team. They will meet you there. And, Diallo, I suggest you all get together with this American film crew and make certain you get their detailed schedule."

To Momar, the last admonishment sounded like a threat, or that the minister was being overly suspicious of the film crew's intentions.

Deciding to escape before the minister could give him more to do, Momar rose and with a quick, "Yes, sir, Mister Minister," he nearly collided with the minister's secretary on the way out the door.

Later, on the way home to pack, he mumbled to himself as he focused on details for the Casamance trip.

In record time his servant had packed a light bag for him. Momar telephoned for his usual chauffeur for the long drive, then gave orders to his servant. He was on his way.

In the car, he smiled and briefly closed his eyes, letting the hum of the car's motor and the comfortable air-conditioning lull him into a light nap.

The chauffeur's slowing down awakened him.

"What is wrong?" Momar mumbled.

"Nothing, sir. Just the annual camel salt caravan, sir."

"*Zut!* That means we will miss the ferry and will have to spend the night at the river."

"Yes, sir," the chauffeur agreed, turning off the air-conditioning when he stopped the car. They immediately felt the result. The car began to heat up rapidly.

"Keep the motor on, damn it!" Momar ordered. The chauffeur complied.

After several minutes, Momar felt foolish because of his outburst. Other people, knowing they would be there for hours, were walking about, visiting and enjoying the spectacle of the several hundred kilometer long caravan. "Oh, never mind," he told the driver as he got out of the car.

Immediately the chauffeur turned off the ignition.

Waves of arid heat shimmered in the distance as Lorraine drove along the almost deserted road approaching Kaolack the next morning. She appreciated that her car was air-conditioned.

Although she had decided to drive to Cap Skirring, she had not yet decided which route to take from Kaolack. She stopped at a gas station, and while the barefoot attendant was cleaning her windshield, she asked his advice. It was hot enough to cook an egg on the body of her car, but she gingerly unfolded her road map over the hood.

"If you take either route, Miss," the attendant told her, "you go through The Gambia to get there. See here though," he pointed a grimy finger at the map, "this green line means that you have to go onto a piste."

"An unpaved road, you mean?" Lorraine asked.

"Yes, miss. But if you take the route that goes through Nioro du Rip, you cross the Gambia River by ferry and the route is paved all the way."

"Yes. I see. Is there another town between Nioro du Rip and Bignona where I could get gasoline?"

"No, miss." The attendant shook his head vigorously.

"You had better fill up my spare gasoline can in that case." She walked around him, opened the trunk of her car and took out a ten-gallon can. He filled and replaced it for her. Lorraine thanked him, and after settling her bill, resumed her journey.

She was complimenting herself on making good time when she saw a long line of stopped cars ahead. "I hope it's not an accident," she said, slowing down. She had been concentrating so much on the traffic ahead that she had stopped behind a car rapide full of people before she saw the longest line of camels she had ever imagined in the world.

"My goodness. What a sight!" she cried, awestruck. She turned off the ignition.

As far as she could see on both sides of the road, nothing but camels, cloaked people, and dust. The adult camels were loaded with sacks, the baby camels trotted alongside on spindly legs, carrying nothing. There were women clad in dark veils and toe-length black djellabas. The men were dressed from head to toe in black with everything covered except for slits, showing dark eyes. Except for being unveiled, the children were dressed like the adults.

As Lorraine stared, she realized suddenly that this must be the ancient salt route that ran from somewhere in black Africa to Arabia. In fact, it had been ancient when Christ was born, she remembered having read. No need to stay in the car, she decided.

Other people in both directions had left their vehicles: the brilliantly-painted car rapides, dilapidated buses, and private cars. No one attempted to disturb the camel caravan crossing their route.

Lorraine left her car and winced at the explosive hotness. It was almost too hot and dry to breathe. She walked to the car that had stopped behind hers.

"Excuse me," she said in French to the young Senegalese couple in it. "Is this the ancient salt route?"

"Yes, it is," the young man answered in the same language.

"There seems to be a lot of them," Lorraine observed, looking at the line of camels and people.

"There is usually more than five thousand in each caravan," the wife supplied. Lorraine's heart sank.

The young husband added, proudly, "These camels have been part of our lives for over three thousand years, miss. Indeed, had it not been for the camel, it would not have been possible to have brought Islam to Sénégal in the twelfth century."

Lorraine suddenly felt as though they were back in the twelfth century as she looked at the curiously dressed people accompanying the endless line of loaded camels and listened to the whoosh, whoosh of the camels' feet. Their hooves sound like whispers in the sand, she thought. To continue her conversation with the young couple, she observed, "They're moving very slowly."

"Yes. Camels always walk slowly," the young wife added, "but they can carry up to five hundred pounds each and walk for three days without water."

The couple had gotten out of their car, and Lorraine was surprised to see them begin to snap pictures. She decided to remain outside her car, too, after she had put on a wide-brimmed straw hat and adjusted her sunglasses. She continued to chat with various people near her.

She was sharing a bottle of water with the young couple and beginning to worry about how late it was getting when a tall handsome man strode up.

"What? What are you, you doing here?" she gasped, almost choking on the water. Momar was the last person she expected to see, though her heart leapt at the sight of him.

"I might ask the same of you," he countered, grinning from ear to ear.

"I'm going to Cap Skirring for a week." She hoped that he would be content enough not to ask any more questions.

Fortunately, he had stopped asking her what she was doing in Sénégal. And since he knew she went to the American Embassy every day and spoke French, he had long ago concluded that she was a new diplomat in spite of her denial that night at the Niani Restaurant.

"I am going to Ziguinchor on a Foreign Office assignment. Yesterday I told you I was on call, remember?"

She nodded, not trusting her voice.

"Well, there is a problem in Ziguinchor that I have to look at," he explained, hoping that he had not sounded as pompous to her as he had to himself.

"I'm beginning to worry because it's nearly sundown and this caravan doesn't show any sign of ending," Lorraine said, turning to look at the scene again.

"It should end in an hour or so," Momar informed her. "My legs were getting stiff sitting in my car so I decided to take a stroll, and who do I find?" he teased, trying to lighten her mood.

Ignoring his bantering, Lorraine wailed, "It will be completely dark by then!"

"Come to my car," Momar invited her. "I will turn on my air-conditioning; and besides, you are getting dusty," he added, grinning again. He was eyeing her white cotton pantsuit that was beginning to darken in some interesting places, he decided.

After she had taken her purse from her car, Lorraine thanked the young couple for the water, locked her car, and strolled alongside Momar toward his.

"My car is one of the first in line, so I will be able to leave as soon as this is over," he told her, guiding her through the people who had gathered in small knots to discuss the camel caravan.

"Nighttime is no time for a woman to drive alone here. Give me your keys. My chauffeur will drive your car," he told her authoritatively. His hand on her arm was beginning to bum her more than the hot sun. She was too hot and tired to protest, though it was her first inclination, considering his authoritative tone.

His chauffeur, having kept an eye out for Momar, turned the ignition back on as soon as he had spied them approaching. He opened the back door of the car for them.

Lorraine almost reeled at the blast of cold air coming from inside. Momar slipped into the car beside her. Noticing that she was shivering, he put an arm around her shoulders and drew her close to him. His nearness made her shake more. She gradually calmed enough to stop shivering.

The chauffeur kept a careful balance with the air-conditioning, turning the motor off to save gasoline, then on again to cool the car. After what seemed like hours to Lorraine, the chauffeur suddenly cried, "Aha! There is the end."

Lorraine stared and was barely able to discern the tail end of the caravan, ghostly now, in the dust-laden twilight.

Momar explained Lorraine's situation to his chauffeur, who hopped from the car, opened the door for Momar, and then moved around the car to open the door on Lorraine's side. She climbed into the front seat, and the chauffeur disappeared toward her car.

They had driven in total silence when Lorraine spotted what looked like stationary fire flies in an even row.

"What's that ahead?" she asked over the hum of the air-conditioning.

"That is the Gambia River ferry crossing. But unfortunately the ferry closes at sundown," he supplied.

She stared at him, her gray eyes huge question marks.

14

In another few minutes, Momar was easing the powerful car to the curb beside an open stall whose shelves held an array of canned goods, straw hats, bags, melons, vegetables, gourds, beer, soft drinks, clothing and live fowl. Lorraine had never seen anything like it. She also saw why the lights resembled fireflies. All the stalls were lit by propane gas lamps. Masses of people surged to and fro.

"Wait here a moment," Momar told her when he cut the ignition. He was back in no time. "We are in luck. My cousin can give us rooms for the night," he said, opening her side of the car.

She was ushered past the array of goods into a back sitting room. An elderly, thin black woman welcomed them in the local language. She offered Lorraine the only chair. Momar told her to take it or the woman's feelings would be hurt. Lorraine sat.

The woman left the room and returned almost immediately with a glass of cool water. Lorraine drank thirstily and gratefully. Her eyes reflected her thanks. The elder woman's black eyes reflected that she understood.

Soon Momar's chauffeur arrived with her luggage. The elderly woman motioned for Lorraine to follow her into a smaller room that contained a bed, a chest of drawers, and nothing else.

While she was getting her bearings, Momar appeared with a white, light-weight cotton djellaba.

"Aicha, my cousin, wants you to have this," he said, handing her the garment.

"I can't accept that," Lorraine cried. "It's from her store. She could sell it."

"Her feelings will be hurt if you do not accept it," he said, pushing the garment toward her.

While they had been talking, a young woman had quietly come in, carrying a huge bucket of water. She was followed by another girl carrying a wash tub, a bar of soap, and a towel. The tub suddenly reminded Lorraine of her grandmother and the old-fashioned wash tubs still at their farm back home in Mound Bayou.

"Dinner is as soon as you are ready," Momar told her before she could protest further.

The young woman motioned to Lorraine that she should follow her to an even smaller room. Once there, she took the tub from the other girl and placed it on the floor. The woman poured the water into it, took the soap and towel from the other girl and passed them to the American. Then they left Lorraine alone.

Lorraine had to admit that the cool water felt great. She slipped on white cotton panties and a bra before donning the djellaba. Like the water, the djellaba felt wonderfully cool to her skin in spite of the warm room. She slipped her feet into a pair of sandals, then combed her long hair. She returned to the sitting room. It had been transformed.

Goat skin poufs and pillows had been placed close to a low, round center table, which was covered with food. Lorraine recognized a roasted chicken, a large piece of roasted lamb, couscous, a vegetable stew, and a variety of soft drinks.

Momar patted the place beside him, indicating that she should sit there. She assumed that he had freshened up in another part of the house because he, too, wore a fresh white djellaba and his hair was wet. A pan of water, soap, and hand towels were passed around. Lorraine gave Momar a questioning look. She had just bathed moments before.

He showed her that she would have to wash her hands again.

Everyone else seated around the table did the same.

When everyone was seated on their haunches around the table, Lorraine saw why she had to wash her hands again. There was no silverware.

Using the fingers of their right hands, everyone tore at the meat and made small wads with the couscous and vegetables. They were experts at getting the food into their mouths, and they laughed good-naturedly at her first aborted attempts. At one point she began to reach out with her left hand but Momar stopped her, whispering that only the right hand was allowed. She had not realized how starved she was until she tried to eat the highly spiced food.

After a few false starts, with everyone laughing, Lorraine quickly learned how to pinch off a piece of her chosen meat, use it to help make a wad with the couscous, gather a vegetable and get it all into her mouth without spilling it.

When the meal was finished, the older woman and the girls quickly removed the remnants of food. They brought in a huge silver-colored charcoal burner, which resembled a samovar. The head of the family, a very old jet-black man, set about preparing the green mint tea, which Lorraine had learned followed all meals. They had already consumed most of the soft drinks with the meal.

The old woman and girls brought in a cone-shaped piece of rock sugar, a tea kettle which they placed on the charcoal burner, a silver tea pot, a tray of small glasses, a bunch of aromatic fresh mint and a tin of tea leaves.

Lorraine watched, fascinated. And in spite of herself, she blushed, remembering the first time Momar had prepared mint tea for her.

While the water was heating, the man picked the mint, leaf by leaf, and placed them in the teapot, his spidery fingers as deft as a woman doing fine sewing. He broke off chunks of the sugar and added them to the tea pot. Lastly, he added the tea.

No one had spoken during these preparations, and Lorraine felt as though it had been a sacred ritual. She almost expected someone to say, "Amen."

Finally, when the water boiled, the old man added it to the tea pot and stirred it a bit. He then left everything to steep. Only then did conversation, in a language Lorraine did not understand, resume. She had the impression that they were teasing Momar about her because whoever was speaking would look timidly at her, then at Momar.

After a few minutes and after everyone had washed their hands again, the old man held the tea pot high over one of the small glasses while the wonderfully perfumed tea streamed into it. He swirled the tea around in the glass, eyed it, tasted it, then poured it back into the tea pot.

"It is not ready yet," Momar needlessly explained. Lorraine was remembering his own tea making ceremony. The women and girls grinned shyly each time she looked at one of them. She was suddenly sorry that she could not speak their language.

When the tea was ready, the old man poured equal amounts into each glass and passed the glasses to his right. The first person on his right passed the glass along until everyone was served.

To her surprise, Lorraine found that the ultra sweet, hot liquid was the perfect ending to the highly spiced meal. For the first time, she did not mind the sweetness. Later, in spite of the heat, Lorraine was asleep almost before her head hit the soft feather pillow on her bed. "Want to take the first ferry?" Momar was shaking her by the shoulder.

At first Lorraine could not orient herself. Then she remembered. "Oh…yes, okay," she slurred, turning over.

"What time is it?" she asked. In the gloom she could make out Momar's face, which was far too close to hers. She wanted him to kiss her.

Instead, he answered her question. "It is six o'clock. The first ferry is in an hour." She was disappointed when he withdrew without another word.

The girls had already brought water for her morning toilette.

When Momar withdrew, she had slid from between the soft sheets and glided to the small anteroom. She stepped into the same tub she had used the night before. She noticed, this morning, that there was a small square hole which was surrounded by porcelain in a corner of the room with a small can of water. She used it. What a relief! Last night she had not noticed it. She stepped into the same tub she had used the night before. And, after cleaning up, she decided to wear the cool djellaba and sandals.

After thanking their hostess and buying a few souvenirs from her, so as not to offend her by offering money for the djellaba, Lorraine headed toward her car.

"My chauffeur will follow us in your car." Momar cut her off.

"Momar, don't be dense. You are on an official mission," she reminded him, adding, "I appreciated last night because it was dark. But today is different," she told him firmly. She was not able to tell what effect her argument was having because his eyes were hidden behind dark glasses to ward off the brilliant sunshine.

She pressed her point. "I insist."

After a moment, he agreed. "All right. But we meet at Cap Skirring," he said firmly. He gave her hands a clasp that created a heat stronger than anything the weather could conjure. But they were too shy to kiss in front of his relatives and other friends who had come to see them off.

A short time later, she wished that she had allowed the chauffeur to drive her car onto the creaking, swaying ferry. But she screwed up her courage and drove ahead, down the steep embankment and onto the ancient contraption, landing among goats, sheep, fowl and crowds of people carrying all sorts of belongings.

She congratulated herself when she arrived at the small, sleepy town of Bignona with its thatched roofed huts and white-washed stone buildings baking in the hot sun. The usual small half-naked children, pecking fowl, and listless dogs were in front of the huts. She knew she was almost at her destination. She tried to ignore Momar's car behind her, which never allowed her out of sight.

When they reached the outskirts of Ziguinchor, Momar's chauffeur tooted the horn as they continued their route, and Lorraine headed for Cap Skirring.

To celebrate being on her own in Sénégal, she turned up the radio as high as the volume would go and stepped on the gas.

"If Andrew could see me now!" She did not know why his name came to mind. She was soaring. But she quickly sobered when, according to the passing road sign, she realized that there were some forty more bumpy, rutted miles to travel before reaching her destination.

15

"It was worth it!" Lorraine cried, stunned at the scene unfolding before her as she drove slowly into the forest of coconut and date palm trees along the wide curving beach.

Club Méditerranée at Cap Skirring lay before her. The central pavilions, tennis courts, swimming pool, boats at anchor, the night club, all came into view as she approached. She slowed as much as possible to take in the sunbathers under colorful parasols; couples strolling along, arm in arm; hammocks slung between palm trees; and gentle waves rolling onto the bleached sands. Lorraine felt her senses spin and soar once more, and she grinned widely.

A short time later she was speaking to the desk clerk, who was dressed in a brightly-colored djellaba. "You have a reservation for Miss Lorraine Barbette." Although her eyes told her that she was in a European resort, Lorraine's mind knew that she was still in Africa, in Sénégal, in Casamance, at Cap Skirring. She was in the home of the Diolas, the Ballantes, the Mandjaques, the Tandas and the Bassaris.

She had done her homework. She knew that the Diolas had objected to this Club, believing it would ruin their paradise.

She also knew they were animists, forest people, secret and dreaming people. That was why she was surprised to see the distinctive Diola features of the desk clerk.

After she had finished registering and received her beads to be used instead of money for all of her purchases, she stowed her suitcase in her room. She now had the difficult decision to make of whether to swim in the pool or the bay. Unable to suppress the euphoric holiday feeling, she said a silent eeny meeny miney moe to help her choose. The swimming pool won.

The delicious water was a touch of paradise as she swam expertly from one end of the pool to the other. She felt alive and vital. With an almost sensual joy, she swam lap after lap in the warm water, totally oblivious to the admiring stares of the men and the envious stares of the women.

Ignoring the gazes of this international crowd, she plopped into a lounge chair beside the pool, giving herself up to the moment.

The sun was already high in the sky when Lorraine woke the next morning. She rolled out of bed and padded to the window. Another glorious day, she thought. She realized she'd been right to take these few days off before finally meeting the film crew's Senegalese escort with Sam and Mark in Ziguinchor.

"But I miss Momar and Micheline," she said aloud.

The shoots around Ziguinchor would be their last, and she wondered what would happen then. She still had not decided what to do about Momar. Her time with him at his relatives made her wonder again about becoming his wife. She liked the idea…a lot. But how did he feel?

"You're here to rest and to enjoy yourself," she reminded herself sternly before shutting off those turbulent thoughts and padding to the bathroom.

Outside, the heat had increased to awesome proportions. Nevertheless, instead of walking toward the swimming pool, Lorraine headed across the burning sands that led to the bay where numerous bathers were cavorting in the shallow water.

The water was calm. Tiny ripples caught the sun and sparkled like a field of diamonds. She wondered how long it would be before Momar came. She missed him terribly, ignoring her own advice to stop thinking about him.

Ziguinchor was hot and humid. Although he had completed most of his work for the Foreign Office, Momar had decided to return to his temporary office. He appreciated the minister's warning about the American film crew, because Momar had additional reasons to believe they were going to try to film the secret ceremonies the coming week. His colleagues, who were part of the escort, had heard rumors, too. He would cross that bridge when he came to it, he decided wearily.

No doubt, there would be trouble. He wished now he had told the minister to find someone else for the escort. He should have gone to Paris. But it was too late for all that now.

His mind went to Lorraine Barbette. He needed time to think. He exhaled slowly, turned his chair and stared out of the window at the shimmering, burnt brown grass beyond. Forest fire conditions, he thought idly. Without Lorraine, he knew he would always feel empty. He knew she might not feel the same way about him. But he didn't care. He needed her. Right now.

His mind made up, he spun the chair back to face his desk. There was nothing to keep him in his office. He thought of Club Med at Cap Skirring with its amusing activities; he thought of the gentle bay breezes; and, most of all, thought about Lorraine Barbette.

Lorraine loved rising early and taking long walks along the edge of the water before the sun began to scorch the land. Her walks were seldom solitary; there were always groups of small children who tagged along. She would chat with them playfully until their mothers or an older sibling would call to them or shyly run up and clutch them. She always enjoyed the children. They reminded her of Mamadou and her own growing desire to have children of her own.

Momar finally arrived, not by road as she had expected, but by water, with a yacht. The man was full of surprises, Lorraine had to admit. She smiled up at him, teasing him with her dove gray eyes. He was steering the big boat away from the quay as if he had sailed such boats all of his life.

He chuckled, and it warmed her. He was as relaxed as she was.

But the heat, which she knew would last all summer, continued unabated. Once they were beyond the bay, however, a breeze swept refreshingly across the deck of the borrowed yacht.

Lorraine knew she could become sunburned, so she slathered on sunscreen lotion generously. Over her bikini, a brief confection of bright red pieces, she wore a pair of loose white pants and matching shirt, which she'd purchased at the Club. The yacht glided along the coast, never out of sight of the many islands that dotted the area. Around them the river glittered like a field of crushed jewels. At one point, they even saw small sharks.

Lorraine screamed when she saw the first shark's fin break through the water's surface. Momar laughed and explained that the sharks around Sénégal were benign, that they had never been known to attack anyone.

When the sun hung straight overhead, a molten copper ball in a colorless sky, Momar dropped anchor in a sheltered bay surrounded by white sandy beaches. The area around Cap Skirring was riddled by such bays, and Lorraine suspected Momar knew them all.

Otherwise, why would he have borrowed his cousin's yacht?

Club Med had packed a picnic lunch for them. They loaded the basket, towels, and Lorraine's beach bag into the rubber dinghy. The bay was so shallow and clear that they could see the sandy bottom clearly.

Once ashore, Momar showed Lorraine how to find clams in the sand with her toes.

"Walk where the sand is wet, dig your toes into it and when you feel a clam, dig it out quickly," he told her, demonstrating the technique for her. He also showed her how to pry oysters from pilings near the shore.

Afterwards, they ate their fill of clams and oysters, which they cooked over a brush fire that Momar made in the sand. They also ate the picnic lunch the Club had prepared. Finally, satiated, they rested quietly on beach towels.

Lorraine asked so quietly that she was almost whispering, "How did you find this place?" She feared disturbing the peacefulness.

Momar misunderstood her motive. His eyes narrowed. "You really mean how many other women have I brought here. Yes?"

Instead of answering, and to convince him of her motive, she ran to the edge of the bay, cupped both hands full of water and threw it at him. Only then did his suspicions vanish. He laughed because most of the water landed on their towels.

He grabbed her by an ankle, forcing her to slowly fall to her knees beside him.

"Think you can read my mind, eh?" she teased.

"I can. Like a book," he bragged. As soon as he released her ankle, she jumped up and ran. He leapt from the towel and ran after her. He threw his towel around her, and instead of releasing her, he reeled her in close, until they were standing only inches from each other.

"But you are not a book, are you, *ma cherie?*"

Her heart caught in her throat. Turning, her voice low and husky, she said, "Momar, is it so hard to understand me? Are you so very different?"

"No," he said quietly. "To both questions." He let go of her and picked up the picnic basket. She followed with the towels, hitching her beach bag over her left shoulder.

The sand at their new location was hot and dry under their sandals, wonderfully clean, washed by the centuries of lapping waves. She dumped her bag in the shade next to the basket, then stepped back to gaze at the nearby palm trees waving their huge branches in the faint breeze. They were as isolated here as they would have been on Mars, Lorraine mused.

She glanced at Momar. He was tugging at the buttons of his jeans. "Shall we swim now that our lunch has digested?"

Her mouth was dry as she watched him slide the jeans down his powerful long legs. She could only nod. Any woman would do anything to have him. Perhaps she was not a fool to be so obsessed with him.

"Anything wrong, *ma cherie?* Too much African sun for you?" He scowled. Without answering, she stripped off her shirt and trousers and tossed them on the sand.

"Last one in is a dead dog!"

"Why such a terrible thing?"

The unexpected question threw her off. He easily outdistanced her, leapt into the water and propelled himself away from the shore.

Later, she tidied up, closed the picnic basket and pushed it to one side of the two big towels. The mid-afternoon sun was hot, but she could think only of their perfect afternoon.

"Need any help?" she asked as he secured the dinghy. She wanted to think only of their perfect afternoon.

"No, thank you. I am finished," he grinned and straightened up.

In a few moments, the yacht skimmed over the smooth water. They motored past several villages with thatched roofs and children and dogs playing along the beaches. She had not noticed all of them on the trip out.

She was surprised at how quickly they arrived at the Club's quay. Momar tossed a line to a young man who secured it with several loops around the huge wooden cleat.

"I'm getting good at getting out of the boat without finding myself between it and the quay," Lorraine laughed as she negotiated the space with quick agility.

"You certainly are." Momar, who was already on the quay, caught her around the waist as she jumped onto it. He held her for an instant, before letting her slide down his body.

"Momar," she said breathlessly, as he ignored the amused stare of the young man and dropped a kiss on her mouth.

"Momar," he mimicked playfully, as the young man said something in a local language. The young man secured the boat. They walked along the beach to where the brightly colored parasols sheltered round tables set out in front of the Club on an expanse of sand as clean and smooth as that of a Japanese garden.

Momar pulled a chair from a table so that she could sit down. He took the seat opposite her.

Twilight found them back in their secret bay. Momar lowered the yacht's anchor into a body of water that shone like glass. Suffused with the orange-red glow of the sunset, the scene was breathtaking. Momar's face was thoughtful as he secured the yacht in preparation for their going ashore.

"Have you thought at all about what it would be like to marry, *ma cherie?*"

The question caught her completely by surprise. She dropped her beach bag abruptly on the deck.

"Well, I, I, uh…" she stuttered.

Momar jerked a rope, the end snapping like a whip.

The sound startled Lorraine.

"Well, I have," he said, moving close to her and caressing her cheek.

"Tell me, *ma cherie,* has whatever it is you do at the embassy taken up so much of your time that you have not seriously considered our relationship?"

"I have been busy, it's true. But I-I wasn't sure you were serious since you haven't mentioned marriage before," she answered lamely. She hesitated, then added frankly, "Maybe I need more time…give it some thought…"

A silence fell between them, and Lorraine was conscious of the deck rocking gently under her sandals. She studied his unreadable face in the dimness of the running light on deck.

When Momar said nothing, she broke the silence. "You've known a lot of women. You still do. Do any of them mean anything to you?"

A suggestion of a smile played around his mouth. "There have not been as many women in my life as you might think. Compared to you, I will be frank with you, they all seem like phonies."

His dark eyes on her were steady, as if gauging her reaction. "I never loved any of them. But I love you, Lorraine."

Lorraine's dove gray eyes widened at his words. It was the first time he had said it—that he loved her. She swallowed, knowing that he was waiting for her response.

"I love you too, Momar," she told him in a whisper, her voice catching. She did love him. So much. But could she marry him? Become his wife? Could their love surmount the gaps between their worlds? Would it be enough of a bridge for them to build a life together?

Lorraine wanted it to be true. She wanted to tell him that she didn't need more time to think about marriage, that she knew this instant she wanted to be his wife. But she had her work and her life back home to think: about. She needed more time to sort it all out…

Momar seemed to see this in her eyes. He said nothing; instead he stepped close and brushed a feather-light kiss across her lips.

Fire raced through her veins at even this brief touch. Oh, how she loved him! How she wanted to be with him forever! Perhaps there was some way they could work it all out.

"Shall we find our way to shore, *ma cherie?*" he asked, his tone promising more of the same smoldering contact she had just briefly sampled.

Lorraine nodded, not trusting her voice. She stooped to pick up part of their gear, and Momar took the beach bag from her. She started down the rope ladder, then began to arrange the equipment in the dinghy as he handed it to her.

When they were ready, he joined her and began to paddle toward the cove where they had been earlier that day. "Why do you return to the same cove when there are so many?" she asked after the long silence between them.

"I like the privacy," he finally replied, his tone husky with wanting. He rested the oars a moment to gaze at her.

She contemplated that for a moment, savoring the heat his gaze sent through her. Adoring the sensation, she hoped that they could come here again before she had to leave Club Med.

"By the way," she said suddenly, "I have to report to work in Ziguinchor on Monday."

"What time do you have to be there?"

"I'll have to arrive about noon."

Neither spoke of work or marriage again that night. Happy for their time together, they both simply enjoyed the romantic evening, carefully avoiding any topic that would spoil the splendid harmony.

16

The Monday morning sun had barely cleared the tops of the palm trees when Lorraine woke with a start. She sat up in bed, rubbing her eyes, her head thick with the need for more sleep. She had lain awake for hours last night after Momar had left on the yacht. She had only dropped off a bit before dawn.

With a groan, she pulled the pillow over her head. Then, dragging herself out of bed, she wandered over to the window. No need to put it off. Today was the day she had to drive back to Ziguinchor, meet her colleagues and their government escort, and begin filming.

"Here's the schedule," Sam said, distributing several stapled sheets of printed material to Lorraine and Mark. "We meet our Senegalese escort at nine tomorrow morning."

Lorraine had arrived, checked into her room and gone to find her colleagues. They were all staying at the same hotel, except for their escorts. The escorts had been lodged elsewhere, she was told. Now she, Mark and Sam were all crowded in Sam's room.

"What about Diop?" Lorraine asked. "Where is he? He'll be able to drive us, won't he?" Lorraine asked.

"Sure. The Foreign Ministry escort will be with us, too, for awhile," Sam said. Lorraine could have sworn that he had a strange light in his eyes when he said that.

Mark had caught it, too, because he shot Sam a perplexed look, which Sam either didn't notice or chose to ignore.

"I thought the diplomatic escort was to be with us for all of our shoots around here," Lorraine interjected, watching Sam closely from where she sat in front of the desk he was using.

"We'll see," Sam answered, a mysterious tone in his voice. He refused to say anything further.

Following the strange meeting, Lorraine took the afternoon off, lounging around the swimming pool.

Promptly at nine the next morning, the film crew was ushered into the local office of the Foreign Ministry to wait for their Senegalese escorts. The secretary seated them around a large round table and offered them a local tea, kinkeliba. Five minutes later, the door opened and in walked Momar, followed by a Senegalese man and woman, whom Lorraine had never seen before. They were all carrying briefcases.

Her mouth flew open, her eyes grew as huge as saucers, and she dropped her glass of tea. Feeling like a total fool, she consciously directed her mouth to close and forced her eyes to shut for a moment. When she opened them, he was still there, moving toward a chair at the table! Lorraine wanted to go through the floor. She wasn't even conscious of the secretary wiping up the spilled tea. She wasn't conscious of her colleagues or of Momar's two colleagues. When she was finally able to speak, she blabbered, "Are you, you, are you…?" She was unable to say anything further.

"And you are the third member of this American film crew?" He was as incredulous as she was. Each one was unaware of the stares of their respective colleagues.

Sam was the first to recover. "Uh, er, Lorraine, this is Mr. Momar Diallo, who is, is our, our…" He stopped, staring from one of them to the other. "Mr. Diallo is the leader of our escorts," he finally got out. The pair had not heard him. They were still too stunned at the turn of events.

Sam decided that it was best to direct his words to the escort members, so he turned to them, saying, "This is Miss Lorraine Barbette, the third member of our team who was out when we met in Dakar. She is the producer and director of our film crew."

The young woman and man acknowledged the introduction.

Gathering up as much dignity as he possibly could, Momar cleared his throat and asked if their briefing could begin. Still shaken, he told them that their orders were to accompany the film crew wherever they wished to film because the local people were more sensitive to foreign film crews than were the people they had filmed in and around Dakar and in Saint Louis. He closed by hoping that the film crew would comply with their orders; and after a few more pleasantries the meeting was over. Momar and Lorraine's colleagues left.

Facing each other across the table, both began to laugh at the same time.

"*You* are the third member of the film crew!" Momar laughed. "And I wondered, after we met your colleagues in Dakar, whether the third member would be a blonde or a brunette." He laughed again. "I was finally convinced that you worked at the embassy in some very sensitive activity."

"And I thought all your work had to do with diplomacy," Lorraine said, giggling.

"What do you mean, diplomacy? Do you not know that one of the most sensitive activities here is seeing that foreign film crews do not insult our people?" he said more sternly than he intended.

"You can be sure that we shall respect the customs of the local people," Lorraine assured him. "After all, we are filming a cultural documentary."

"I am certain that I can trust you, but nevertheless, you understand our position. We must accompany you on all of your filming here," Momar said quietly, but firmly.

"Yes. I understand and appreciate it," Lorraine answered, just as quietly.

"What are we waiting for? Shouldn't we follow them if we don't want to get lost?" Lorraine asked as she, Sam, Mark and Diop stood outside their hotel near the minivan and saw their escort pulling away in the ministry car.

"Yes," Mark agreed. "Shouldn't we, Sam?"

He cast them both a scowl. "I wish the two of you wouldn't bug me so much. They have gotten used to us pulling out after them, and the traffic isn't so heavy that we are likely to lose them," he said, casting an eye at the bumper-to-bumper downtown traffic passing in front of their hotel. "Besides, I told them that we would meet them at the filming site," Sam added.

"We'll lose them this time if we don't hurry," Lorraine exclaimed as though Sam had not spoken.

With an ambling gait that Lorraine and Mark both found frustratingly slow, Sam struggled into the minivan. He paused for a long time and surveyed his two anxious colleagues.

"We *can't* lose them since they'll be waiting for us at the site," he repeated, trying to put them at ease. "We can start now," he said, glancing at his wristwatch. "Hop in." He stepped away from the door to make room for them.

Diop jumped into the driver's seat and they slammed all the doors shut and headed into the traffic on the road leading to the town of Bignona, beyond the bridge over the Casamance River. But that was the opposite direction!

Lorraine leaned forward, "Diop, do you know where our escort is headed? Why are you taking us in the opposite direction?"

Diop did not answer. Lorraine and Mark gave each other anxious looks. Sam snickered. The silence was deadly.

A short time later, Diop pulled off the road sharply at an approaching dirt track, leading into the forest bordering the road.

Only then did Sam break the heavy silence. "We know where we're going, don't we, Diop?" he asked, winking at the driver, who gave a shaky smile in acknowledgment.

Mark, who hadn't missed Sam's wink, asked in an ominously quiet voice, "So where are we going, Sam?"

After a long pause, Sam deigned to answer. "We're going about twenty kilometers east of Ziguinchor, where there is a sacred forest. There is an initiation ceremony taking place tonight. Diop happens to know where it is."

"Diop?" Lorraine and Mark asked in unison. Diop nodded and grinned, proud to be the center of attention, it seemed.

"You know those ceremonies are secret and closed, not only to foreigners but to women, as well!" Lorraine cried, horrified, frightened, and furious. Overcoming her horror and sudden disgust, she asked angrily, "How did you learn about such a ceremony anyhow?"

Sam did not answer right away. When he did, his voice was guarded. "I made a few friends at the Ministry of Foreign Affairs when I was over there these past few weeks. And Diop here is cooperating with me. One of my friends contacted us last night with the details of tonight's ceremony."

"I can't believe this!" Lorraine exploded, angrier and more afraid than she had ever been in her entire life.

Mark's mouth was hanging open. He was speechless.

Diop pressed harder on the accelerator. They were deep in the forest now. The track became narrower and more full of potholes. Lorraine scowled and spat at Diop, "So then you, you knew about this?"

"Yes, miss," he admitted with a sheepish grin.

"How did you bribe people at the ministry into giving you this information, Sam?" Lorraine asked angrily, trying to stifle her fear. *Oh, God,* she thought. *Heaven help us!* Sam smiled for the first time. "In this business, it's easy to pay off people."

Lorraine wanted to dig a big hole and escape into it. She wanted to be anywhere except where she was. She felt like a trapped animal. After the promises she had made to Momar and his ministry. To be part of this! If only there was some way she could escape, but that was out of the question now.

It was too late to try to escape. It was growing dark and they were miles from any kind of habitation. She was trapped.

Unknown to her, Mark was going through the same kind of torture. His first reaction had been, "I'll be damned if I'll film such a ceremony." But, after thinking for awhile, he decided that his only recourse would be to try to escape. But he wouldn't leave Lorraine alone with these crooks, he thought angrily but silently. He kept his thoughts to himself.

The drive to the sacred forest took about thirty minutes more, during which time everyone was silent, enveloped in their individual thoughts.

Sam was ecstatic. He never would have believed, in his wildest dreams, that it would be so simple to lose the escort and to find the sacred forest.

Diop was already counting the francs he would receive and happy that he would soon be able to pay the bride price to Assitou's father. Diop finally slowed down. He pulled into a small clearing and came to a full stop at the foot of a giant baobab tree. "Why are we stopping here?" Lorraine asked anxiously, more frightened than ever.

Sam gave her a nasty look. "The sacred place in the forest is about a quarter of a mile from here. We'll go the rest of the way on foot." He took a tight hold on her arm. There was no way to escape him.

Diop brought up the rear with Mark behind Lorraine and Sam on the narrow trail. Lorraine's legs were rubbery. She wondered how she was able to put one foot in front of the other.

"Courage, my dear," Sam said nastily when she hesitated briefly.

Lorraine felt like spitting in his face. How could she and Mark have been so blind? This was what Sam obviously had referred to back in Dakar at the meeting when he had said that they would be rich and famous. Rich and famous indeed! They would be lucky if they came out of this alive! Lorraine thought to herself with growing alarm.

The government won't lift a hand to save us if we are caught by the people in charge of this secret ceremony, Lorraine thought, fear taking over. *We will be lucky if we are simply expelled from the country. We could be killed!*

Lorraine stumbled, almost falling. Sam gave her arm a sharp jerk. She stopped, whirling on him, and spat, "I hope a black mamba snake bites you!"

"Be quiet!" Sam snarled. "You're bluffing anyway."

Nevertheless, he shone his flashlight into the dense forest where the vine-wreathed trees stood like ghosts. The light hardly pierced the dense darkness in front of them and quickly faded in the thick blackness. It was still, hot, and omniously silent. Lorraine's heart seemed to stop.

The usual noise of night birds screeching and crickets chirping had gone silent because of the intruders. "There are no black mambas in forests," Diop murmured. "She's lying."

They continued on into the hot lush blackness, all of them nearly falling several times. They passed other giant kapok trees, and lush tropical trees that Lorraine was unable to identify along the well-trodden trail on into the hot lush blackness.

"Damn!" Sam hissed, and stopped so suddenly that Lorraine almost fell. "What was that?" he whispered, swinging the flashlight wildly.

"What?" Diop was saying, pushing Mark into Lorraine. "What did you see, Sam?" Even Diop was beginning to get nervous.

"I-I don't know," Sam's voice was shaky.

Lorraine hoped it was a monkey or some other small animal.

It turned out to be a palmist, a rat-like creature that lives on wild palm trees. Sam's hand was biting deeper into her arm. She was learning fast that Sam could be a cruel man. Fear, she learned, had hands of steel, like Sam's hands felt on her arm. But she would fight that fear. She must stay calm.

"Sam! We can't go in there!" Mark protested, stumbling as Diop gave him a slight push toward where they could hear drumming sounds in the distance.

"We have some friends there," Sam shot over his shoulder, never letting up the pressure on Lorraine's arm.

"You don't have to break my arm, Sam," Lorraine finally said when she was sure she could control her voice. "You know as well as I do that I would be crazy to try to escape in this forest." She shrugged angrily when he complied.

"But no funny business, you two," he ordered savagely.

"If those people spot us, they aren't going to be very pleased, to say the least," Mark growled.

"That's a problem we'll solve when the time comes," Sam told him curtly. "So, just shut up and don't try anything foolish."

They were close enough now to hear the constant drumming.

Sweat broke out all over Lorraine's body with each beat of the tam-tams—the sick, clammy sweat of fear. She wondered if Mark was as scared as she was.

"If all goes well, we'll have our film and be out of here within an hour," Sam continued, as though they were going to shoot a legitimate film.

"If all goes well," Lorraine added sarcastically.

They were stumbling along through thicker and thicker vegetation. It grew darker until the moon rose and they were able to see a few feet ahead.

Sam suddenly stopped. Or, Lorraine hoped, he was just scared. "Diop, let's change places," said Sam. "You lead." They changed places with Diop also carrying most of the film gear.

Suddenly, Lorraine was beset with an alarming thought. She might never see Momar again; and if she did, he would never believe that she had not been in on this.

He would likely believe that this was the very reason she had kept her job a secret from him. Or worse, he might conclude that their whole relationship was a scam, that she had somehow wanted to use him to gain this film footage. This trip had quickly turned into a nightmare, and she was certain it was not over yet.

They rounded a bend and she could make out a series of much taller trees in the distance, off to their right.

Diop signaled for them to stop. He dropped the film gear and slipped into a heavily wooded area, heading for the nearest big tree. Once there, he cupped his hand over his mouth and emitted a high screeching monkey sound. A moment later, he received an answering screech from a point deeper in the forest. *Good,* he thought a bit nervously, *our friends are in place.* He returned to tell the film crew. They had reached their destination.

They worked their way stealthily toward the farthest big tree. Sam and Diop checked the branches of each tree on the chance that the ceremonial officials had posted sentries.

They approached their target tree cautiously. "Why are we stopping here?" Lorraine whispered, conscious of the danger.

Sam gave her a stern look. "The ceremony will take place just beyond those tall bushes, in that clearing," he snapped. Diop slid up a nearly invisible rope ladder that had been placed for them. Sam signaled for Lorraine and Mark to follow Diop.

At the top of the tree was a blind, the kind hunters use. A straw mat covered the floor and a hole had been made in the blind that overlooked the ceremonial grounds, which were visible about a hundred feet away. The smell of stale wood and straw hung in the still air inside the blind. It was hot, damp and full of noisy mosquitoes.

Diop began to set up the tripod and one of the cameras. Then Sam and Diop conferred near the hole in the blind. Afterward, Sam ordered, "Help him set up that camera, Mark. Don't just stand there!" Then he added, "And don't do anything stupid."

Resigned to his fate, Mark made himself handle the expensive equipment. He had loaded the two cameras back in Ziguinchor. "What a damned fool I am!" he spat under his breath. He and Lorraine had fallen completely into Sam's trap. He had been fool enough to even mount a high speed telephoto lens on the camera they were setting up. He had added dry cell batteries to the sack and four hundred extra feet of film. While he had been looking after loading the cameras, Lorraine had loaded the Nagra recorder using a very delicate microphone to minimize the recording noise. She checked its boom and headphones. And, because they had already done some night filming, they knew the nights in Sénégal were humid. They wrapped a heavy blanket around the cameras to protect them. Now Mark felt like the world's biggest scared fool!

It was unbelievable, Lorraine thought, swallowing the huge lump in her throat. Sam was a colleague of theirs, a man she had worked with these past five years. And now, he had become an enemy. Simply because of his greed. Just how well did she know this—this…She was unable to finish the sentence.

Lorraine glanced at Mark, who was standing in front of the hole in the blind, peering into the darkness, wondering about his future, or maybe he was wondering if he had a future. She saw that sweat was running down his face.

All right, Lorraine thought. Sam had not been a very close colleague. Not as close as Mark had been. Maybe his turning from colleague to enemy could be understood. Maybe he had debts she did not know about. Maybe he was a secret gambler. Then again, she mused, maybe he was just plain greedy.

Lorraine thought she should try to persuade Sam to change his mind and not go through with this crazy thing. "Sam, it's not too late to change plans. Let's return to the hotel. Tell our escort that we got lost. You don't have to go through with this," she concluded, knowing before she stopped talking that she wasn't getting through. But she continued, "Come on, Sam."

"Look, Lorraine," he said, his tone harsh, "I promised myself that one day I would be rich. I'm not a young man and I have to take charge of every chance I can get. This is my big chance."

"You're greedy."

"You're right. Somebody who once worked on Wall Street said that greed was the first law of getting rich," Sam smirked. "So, don't waste your breath."

The moon had gradually risen above the tall trees, casting an eerie almost early daylight haze into the clearing beyond their hiding place. Lorraine sighed, fighting her sick fear.

She noticed that Mark had sat back on his haunches. She wondered what he was thinking.

After a while, a masked man entered the glade. He was garbed in a cascading cape that fell to the ground. It was decorated with multi-colored streamers from the top to the hem. He also wore an animal mask on his head. From where the crew hid, it was difficult to distinguish his features. The glade quickly filled with other masked individuals. They were followed by musicians, who joined the tam-tam players, their black upper bodies gleaming with sweat. The masked persons began a slow shuffling dance, forming a circle.

Sam ordered Mark to begin filming.

Lorraine felt sick with fear and loathing, yet she almost reminded Sam that she was their director. She nearly laughed hysterically. There was no way she would give orders to film this ceremony.

Mark had placed himself behind the camera; he was wondering how he could spoil the film without Sam noticing.

Lorraine moved to Mark's side as if to begin directing. Instead, she squeezed his hand, saying nothing. He took that as a signal to do something. He didn't know what, but he had a feeling something was about to happen. ·

"Sam, why don't you and Diop take the second camera and get closer up. That way we can be out of here sooner," Mark suggested, hoping against hope that Sam wouldn't detect the tremor in his voice, or become suspicious at the suggestion. He was counting on Sam's greed.

When Lorraine squeezed his hand tighter, Mark knew that he had said the right thing.

Mark knew from his research that the masked dancers would become more frenetic as the evening wore on and as other dancers joined the group. They would be dressed in long metal leg ringlets, with waistbands of woven metal and more ringlets with lightly woven bands of cloth holding them up. Aside from their tasseled headbands, those strange metal ringlet costumes were just about the only thing the men would be wearing. Then the initiates would arrive, their only clothing head covers. This was no place for a woman, and a foreign woman, at that.

Mark became livid when he remembered how Sam had practically drooled over the displays at the Ifran Museum back in Dakar. He had guessed right. Sam's greed had taken over.

"Think you can work the camera, Diop?" Sam asked the chauffeur.

"Sure," Diop answered, grinning and mentally counting his francs.

"Then, what are we waiting for?" Sam asked, fairly gloating. He quickly assured himself that Mark and Lorraine were trapped and far too scared to move from the blind while he and Diop were gone.

They scrambled down the rope ladder. Mark and Lorraine could barely see them as they slipped noiselessly away. A moment later, Lorraine dangled the minivan's keys in front of Mark's face. "Look!" she cried. But she didn't have to tell him because Mark's eyes were already huge.

"How did you manage that?" Mark asked, incredulous.

"While Diop was setting up the tripod, when he stooped over, I slipped them out of his pocket," Lorraine said, smiling nervously but for the first time since their ordeal had begun.

"Let's give them three minutes then get out of here while we still have our skins," Mark whispered, still very nervous.

"If we want to move fast, we'll have to leave the equipment," he added sadly, literally caressing the camera on the tripod.

"I know, but we have no choice," Lorraine said, her voice ready to crack.

"Can you run fast?" Mark asked, to pass the time.

"As fast as you, I think. I have on tennis shoes and I work out regularly," Lorraine replied.

"Then let's go. I'll help you down." Once on the ground, neither of them looked back as they slipped silently away.

Or so they thought.

They had not gone fifty yards before Lorraine saw the jet black man blocking their path! Horrified, Lorraine watched as he rushed toward them. His black eyes were like ebony stones. Lorraine's brain churned as she clutched at Mark for support.

They were done for! Far from civilization, it would happen nice and clean with that evil-looking machete-like weapon the man was brandishing at them now. He could kill them and bury their bodies or leave them for the hyenas, and no one would ever find them. In silence the man, who wore a skimpy loin cloth and nothing else except the machete-like weapon, signaled them to get in front of him. He pushed them deeper into the forest, in the opposite direction they had taken. Lorraine cast around trying to remember landmarks. She had better think, she told herself, as terrified as she was.

Her mind functioned enough for her to remember that her grandmother, who was half Choctaw Indian, used to take her into the forest in Mississippi and show her how to track and how to identify wild edible and medicinal plants.

Suddenly Mark groaned, and he was brought back with a jerk to their situation. "Jesus, what a mess we're in now!" he whispered. "Caught like monkeys in a trap."

They trudged on.

"You all right?" Mark asked her at one moment.

The African man prodded them along and growled something neither of them could understand.

The forest around them was hot and humid, and mosquitoes swarmed about their unprotected heads. In some places, ripples of moonlight shone through, but the two prisoners were in no mood to contemplate it. What they did notice were the black shadows and huge tree trunks. When they could, they gazed at the star-filled sky and the moon.

When Lorraine glanced at her wristwatch, she was amazed to realize that they had been traveling a half hour. Their guard signaled to them to turn off the trail they had been following. There was little undergrowth here, making it easier to move.

Lorraine watched very carefully to remember land marks. Where the hell was he taking them? To the killing ground, if such a place existed. And Lorraine didn't doubt for a moment that there was such a place.

Then she and Mark saw it at the same time. A blot of blackness darker than the night. They both stopped. The hut, a small round thatched affair, had no lights, and there was no movement near it.

Was this where they would be executed? Put to death? She wondered what was to happen to them. Was Mark thinking the same thoughts as she? She was afraid to look at him.

No, I will not die! There is only one slim chance of getting out of this and as soon as I can communicate with Mark, we have to try it. Before they were hustled into the dank smelling hut, Lorraine found it. The depression in the ground and a brush fence which faced the depression could be used for cover. It would do. She had quickly measured the distance in relation to the door of the hut. It might work. It might give them a fifty-fifty chance of escaping. Besides, she noticed, no one else joined their captor. They probably thought he could handle two very frightened unarmed Americans, especially since one of them was a reed-thin slip of a girl.

They both sighed together when their captor had pushed them into the dark, stinking hut and slammed the door. They heard him slide a bar across it from the outside.

Lorraine swallowed, took a deep breath and said so quietly that he had a problem hearing her, "Mark, I have a plan."

He waited silently while she explained.

They heard a rustling sound from outside. They both froze. Then they heard their captor stride off.

Lorraine and Mark had been in enough straw huts since coming to Sénégal to have an idea of their construction. Although it was night, they felt around until they found a stool. They bumped into each other often in the dark hut.

Mark spoke. "Let me climb onto the stool, Lorraine, because there might be snakes or scorpions in the beams." Lorraine shivered. She was scared to death of snakes. And she had no love for scorpions, either. But this would be their only chance. If it worked.

As soon as he had climbed up and his eyes were even with the place where the thatch roof met the wall, Mark could discern slight rays of moonlight.

Pulling frantically at the thatch, he grew sweaty with the effort, and sweatier from fright. What if their captor returned with reinforcements before they had a chance to escape? Dust and dry thatch rained down on Lorraine, who was too frightened to move aside.

At last, it seemed like a century, Mark had made a hole large enough to poke his head through. Slowly, he lifted himself high enough to peer around. No one was in sight. Their captor must have gone for reinforcements. So the faster they escaped, the better. Quickly, Mark dropped back to the floor to whisper to Lorraine that both must escape by the hole he had made, leaving the barred door intact.

Mark made the hole big enough to squirm through. Then he whispered to the frightened young woman to mount the stool and to raise her hands toward him. She was too frightened to do otherwise. Mark stood and pulled her out.

Once they were both on the roof, they dropped easily to the hard packed earth and ran quickly to the depression Lorraine had seen earlier. That way they could see anyone approaching on the trail without being seen.

After taking only a moment to catch their breath, Mark quietly rasped, "Run, Lorraine, let's run!" Then he grabbed her arm, dragging her along.

"This way," he said, heading in the opposite direction from which they had come.

"Oh, Mark!" Lorraine was crying now. "Oh, my God, Mark. What are we going to do? How could we have landed in such a mess!"

"It's okay. We're safe for the time being."

"Oh! Oh! I hear them coming!" Lorraine said, pulling at Mark's arm, digging her fingers into his skin.

Something in Mark righted itself then, an instinct, the need to survive. He led them farther into the forest, running bent over, not sure they were still being pursued but not stopping to find out either.

Mark could hear Lorraine's labored breathing above his own.

"Are you all right?" he asked once.

"Yes," she answered breathlessly.

They ran on, leaving the hut far behind, sweating, gasping, dodging trees and vines, and tripping over they didn't know what.

And they kept going, toward the night, lost in the deep forest of Casamance, in Sénégal, in Africa! Running, running into the dank, mosquito infested, humid night.

17

"The moon is directly above us now," Lorraine said, leaning against an ancient tree to rest.

"And we can make better time because we can see better where we're going," Mark added. He had crouched on his haunches, resting, too.

"We can make better time, but then so can they," Lorraine observed. "And, don't forget they know this forest."

"Do you think they're close?" she asked.

He stood and shrugged. "Maybe we'd better move on." He peered at her. "Are you all right?"

They moved on through the forest, avoiding worn paths and animal trails, keeping to the dense foliage for cover. The forest took on an eerie, magical look, a murky haze, though it was still dark. In Sénégal, Lorraine observed crazily, one minute it was dark, the next minute bright daylight. As they moved deeper into the forest, sometimes a twig would snap and both would stop and listen, but there was only a deathly silence.

They moved as if by some dark magic, and the moonlight reached out to lead them astray, confusing them.

They had intended to circle back to the minivan. Although it was too risky to go to it, they knew they could at least begin to parallel the road they had taken into the forest. It would lead them to the Bignona route and eventually back to Ziguinchor. Then what?

"Are you certain this is the way?" Mark asked Lorraine, stopping in the now brilliant moonlight penetrating the dense trees.

She gazed around, trying to orient herself, calling upon all of her Indian blood and her grandmother's training.

"I...I think it is, Mark."

The forest animals began to stir. Birds they could not see sang to one another, green and red parrots flew overhead. Monkeys chattered. But the feeling in the air was not right, Lorraine felt. As humid and sultry as it was, there was no mist clinging to the forest floor.

They stopped in a glade by a brook and cupped their hands, drinking the clear water, not allowing themselves to imagine the chance they were taking. Their malaria pills were back at the hotel. Besides, Lorraine observed silently, if they were caught, malaria would be the least of their worries.

"We had better move quickly," Lorraine told Mark.

It was an hour later when Lorraine finally gave up, stopped and slumped to the ground, ready to cry. "Tired?" Mark asked, squatting beside her.

"Yes. I'm tired. I'm hungry and I'm scared, and..."

"And what?"

"I think we're lost."

"Lost?" Mark echoed, his mouth hanging open.

"Lost. So much for my Indian blood and forest knowledge."

"But how?"

"Look," Lorraine said, sitting up, "I don't know this forest at all. If we were on a path, but this…" she indicated the dense growth surrounding them.

"What do you think then?"

She sighed. "I think we're headed in the general direction of Ziguinchor. We're looking for the Bignona route, but it seemed to me we should have crossed it."

"So, what do we do now?"

"Rest," Lorraine said tiredly. "If we don't rest for awhile we'll never get out of here. We had better eat some of the edible things I've noticed."

"Like what?" Mark asked, looking around.

"Like this monkey bread here," she said, bending to pick up a large green fuzzy pear-shaped cone that had fallen from a baobab tree nearby. She showed Mark how to break it open to reach the cream colored pulp inside.

"Where did you learn about this?" Marked wanted to know.

"I have seen the children eating them. And I have seen them on sale at the Sandaga Market. They are used to make beverages," she told him. She added, after a while, "When the leaves are dried and pounded into a powder, the cooks use them in Senegalese couscous, too."

They moved fast after that short rest. Lorraine was hoping and praying that they were on the right track, going toward the Bignona route. If they could find it, they could hitch a ride. *Sure, with the police,* a little voice told her. She was certain the police would arrest them, if their pursuers didn't find them first.

The going seemed to get rougher and hotter. After all, it was Sénégal, Lorraine thought. It was deathly still again. The animals seemed to have gone into hiding. They had gone silent. Sweat ran down Lorraine's neck and face and wet her dirty tee shirt and jeans. Mark's tee shirt and jeans were also soaked through. They found another stream and drank thirstily. This time malaria pills were absent from their thoughts. It was too hot to talk.

Lorraine licked her dry, cracked lips and felt her thighs and legs tremble. Shielding her eyes, she stopped to get her bearings. The moon should be to our right, she knew. If they were heading in the right direction, that is.

"Are you certain the road is in front of us?" Mark had asked several times.

"I'm almost certain," was all Lorraine was willing to admit.

They had not heard any sign of their pursuers, but they were not taking any chances, either. Every time they had to cross a clearing, they bent double and ran, panting, thirsty, hungry and bone tired. The moon dipped below the tree tops and the hot air remained still. Too still.

Lorraine stopped, plopped down and mopped at her face with the bottom of her tee shirt. Instinctively she looked west. The moon had almost disappeared, but there was a strange glow above the trees. Strange. She had never seen such redness at night during all the time she had been in Sénégal. And it should be cooler and that strange glow remained.

"We aren't lost, Mark," Lorraine suddenly announced.

Mark stopped. "You mean you know where we are?"

She pointed. "See that huge baobab over there? I'm certain it's the one we passed in the minivan, coming in here."

"That's good to know," Mark said. "You know we could have ended up in the Gambia if it hadn't been for you."

"Well, we would have had to swim the Gambia River first," Lorraine added with a sardonic smile. Then she reached out and gave his arm a small squeeze.

She sniffed the air. So did Mark. Something smelled strange.

"Do you smell something?" Mark asked.

"You too? Yes, I do. What do you think it could be?" Lorraine asked, puzzled.

Then she turned toward the western sky.

"Oh, my God!" she whispered, horrified.

Mark looked where she was staring.

"They have set the forest on fire to flush us out!" Lorraine cried.

"We're finished, and just when we were so close," Mark said.

"I'm scared." Lorraine cried, horrified.

Mark was struck dumb.

Lorraine had to say something to prevent panic in both of them. "We can't give up now, let's get going."

"I just hope we get out of this alive." Sometime later, Mark's face was as dirty and sweaty as Lorraine's. He was even getting a growth of beard. She had never seen Mark with a growth of beard before. He didn't say anything, and she wondered what he was thinking. *What would they do if they got out of this mess? Maybe they wouldn't get out.*

Lorraine tripped on something and fell. She held back the tears that threatened. The heat was overwhelming, and they could see smoke behind them. Mark was beside her immediately, his brown eyes concerned. "Are you hurt?" he asked, sitting on his haunches.

"No, I'm all right." She wiggled her toes in the badly scuffed tennis shoes. "We should reach the road soon."

They had to go on. They had to…

Mark took off his tee shirt.

Momar sat on the bed in his hotel room and tried to think calmly. He had sent the two other members of the escort team off to bed. At least someone should rest, he thought. He tried to force himself to eat the meal he had ordered from room service, but he had no appetite.

For the life of him, he could not figure out what had happened with that American film crew. It was as if they had disappeared into thin air. But he had his suspicions.

It had been hours since the escort had returned to the hotel when they had realized that the film crew was long gone. What were they up to? Where were they? Someone had told them that they had seen the minivan on the Bignona route. The escort had driven along there, looking around. Nothing.

He could not believe they had gotten lost. No way. Diop knew the area well, and that Sam person had gone with Momar to show him where the crew would be filming. The only thing he could do now was wait.

It must have been another hour before Momar stood, stretched and peered out the window. The moon had risen, a full moon, he noticed absently. Its brilliance threw shadows on the building across the street, and Momar remembered his and Lorraine's last day at beach at the bay.

He wondered if Lorraine was safe. Momar paced his room restlessly. He peered out the window again, alert at every sound. He was expecting the film crew to pull up in front of the hotel at any moment.

Momar returned to the window. Outside, the moon was illuminating the scene in front of the hotel in near brilliant detail. Nothing moved, not even a stray dog. *Where are they?*

Momar returned to sit on the bed. He rubbed the stubble on his chin with a shaky hand. It was going to be a long night.

The telephone rang, sounding like a screaming hyena. Momar's muscles spasmed. He was certain that it was Lorraine telephoning to tell him that they had gotten lost, that the van's tire had a blowout.

He reached for the telephone, picked it up, held it to his ear. "Momar Diallo here," he said.

"Monsieur Momar Diallo?" came a voice he did not recognize. Not Lorraine's. A man's voice, a stranger's voice. "Monsieur Momar Diallo who is in charge of the escort team for an American film crew?"

Momar's heart froze. "Monsieur Diallo, I am in charge of the initiation ceremonies in the sacred forest just north of Ziguinchor. Are you there?"

Momar's hand gripped the receiver so tight that his knuckles hurt. "Yes, I am here." He could hardly breathe.

"We have caught some foreigners trying to film the ceremonies."

Momar's whole body was suddenly paralyzed, a terrible choking numbness, then numbing fear, then monumental rage at his stupidity. "Repeat that," he choked.

The voice on the other end of the line did. "We have a mulatto woman and a white man."

Momar stood beside the bed, his head bowed, shoulders slumped, hand tightly holding the telephone. His mind raced like a scared monkey swinging from tree to tree.

Lorraine! They had Lorraine! He did not give a damn about anyone else. But Lorraine! How she had deceived him! Pretending to be so sincere. So alluring. So beautiful. She had done it. He had never suspected.

They could kill her. And he would be responsible. Not only had he failed to protect his countrymen from violation, but worse, he had failed to protect the woman he loved. He could not live with that. He could not survive it.

"All right. What do you want me to do?" He finally asked. He could hear the caller breathing into the mouthpiece.

"Do you know the clearing where we do the actual circumcisions?" the caller asked.

"Yes," Momar answered.

"We will be bringing the woman and man there at daylight. You and the police can come for them then," the man spat into the mouthpiece.

"All right. We will be there," Momar answered, sick. "I advise you: Do not harm them," he tried but knew his words mattered little.

They should all have been safely back here, in bed! That was all Momar could think. But this was not the time for that, and that's what mattered now.

Momar clutched the telephone for dear life and felt a knot of sick rage tie up his stomach. He put the telephone down, very carefully, as if by doing so he was protecting Lorraine in some way. He stood there, head down, arms hanging loosely, staring at the telephone as if it were a black mamba, Sénégal's deadliest snake. Hate filled him, squeezing his insides like a python squeezes its victims. He feared for the woman he loved, Lorraine Barbette. Hopelessness almost swept him away, then resolve took over.

He knew what he had to do. He had to get to the bottom of this monumental mess.

No sense waiting until morning. No sense in waking the other members of the escort team. He grabbed his car keys and strode out the door. And all the time his mouth was as dry as the sands around Tambacounda and his heart was pounding like the ceremonial tam-tams at a circumcision ceremony. "Lorraine, *ma cherie*, is in danger. I have got to save her, no matter what."

Why was she mixed up in this? Was she afraid? Was she hurt?

Momar drove along the Bignona route. His mind worked from time to time, now concentrating on the road, now on Lorraine, seething with anxiety. His car's headlights swung wildly across the wall of thick foliage that bordered the narrow pock-marked forest. It all seemed to be closing in on him even before he reached the turn off the film crew had taken. He jerked the steering wheel when he suddenly came upon the turn off. It seemed like a century later when he came upon the minivan. He pulled up in front of it, turned off his car's motor and left the keys in the ignition.

It was eerily quiet, hot, and humid. He needed no light because the moon was still bright and, besides, he had been a *selbé,* or mentor, to several young boys being circumcised here since his own initiation.

What would he say when they arrived in the morning? A million things went through his mind as he walked, but none of them would work.

For hours Momar had fought to avoid panicking. He kept reminding himself that he was a diplomat, accustomed to handling delicate and difficult situations.

He knew the forest well. He headed for the circumcision site. No one. The air smelled of smoke but that was normal, he surmised. The doctor would need fire to heat the circumcision instruments. But what he smelled was stronger than a leftover fire.

Momar, nevertheless, stared at the place where the big fire was only a few cinders now.

He could picture the scene. The djembes or tam-tams would set the rhythm. The head organizer would arrive first, to the sound of tam-tams, with his mask and long decorated robes. He would set the dancing pace and the other dancers would follow. Lastly, the boys to be circumcised would enter the glade, naked except for their head coverings of sacks to prevent them from recognizing any place and to prevent them from seeing where the sacred instruments were hidden.

Each boy would be led by a father, an uncle, an older brother, or a very good friend of the family. The secret amulets would be brought out and blessed by an elder, so designated because of his wisdom and knowledge and his standing in the community.

Once the fire had died down and while the embers remained red hot, the doctor would place the knife of hammered steel there until it was red hot.

In the meantime, another doctor would have had the *selbé,* or mentor line the boys up. Then the doctor would tie the tip of each boy's male member with a plaited hair from a horse's mane.

Momar could still feel, in his imagination, when the doctor had tied his. However, since his *selbé* had had both hands on his tiny shoulders, to encourage him, he, like his circumcision mates, had refused to cry out.

He had not cried out when the doctor sliced off the tip because by then the horsemane had been tied so tight that there was no more feeling. They had danced to the hypnotic music of the *djembés* and then they had been led away, deep into the forest to be dressed in new white boubous and to receive other secrets that would aid them to become men.

They would remain in the forest for two weeks, learning how to behave with girls, how to forage for food, how to hunt, how to become a man.

The heat. Momar could still feel it now, after all these years. Yet the air smelled much too strongly of smoke. Momar shook his head as though in a stupor. Not only was the smoke stronger but the heat was much hotter.

"Zut!" Momar swore. While he had been lost in memories, there was a real fire, and it was getting closer to where he was standing.

18

"Oh, Mark, how did we end up in this terrible situation? What a mess!" Lorraine cried, trying hard not to become hysterical.

"Funny, I would never have suspected that Sam would do such a thing," Mark mused, as though talking to himself.

They stumbled on. Onto the road!

They had only walked a few hundred yards when the truck driver saw them: Two filthy foreign apparitions stumbling along as though there were drunk.

He slammed on the brakes. His truck came to a screeching stop. He leaned out the windowless door and surprised them by asking in French, "Are you people lost?"

Lorraine answered that their car had broken down and they needed a ride to Ziguinchor. The driver explained that he was only going to the central market with his vegetables and fowl and a lamb.

They were so grateful that they hadn't run into the police or their pursuers or that the fire hadn't reached them that they weren't about to complain to the driver. They squeezed into the antiquated vehicle. Mark closed the door and they rattled off, the truck sputtering, coughing and jerking before it picked up a bit of speed.

Lorraine mentioned the fire to the driver. She had to yell over the noisy motor. "Just someone burning off the undergrowth," he replied. "We farmers do it all the time this time of year. It is going to rain any moment, and it will put out the fire," he yelled back.

Lorraine and Mark looked at each other, wanting to believe him.

At the market they thanked him profusely. Lorraine was in a daze but now was not the time to give up. She hung onto Mark. She almost collapsed when they left the truck. Mark held her up, his arm under hers.

"Are you all right?" he asked for the umpteenth time.

"I'll be okay. Just a reaction, I guess. We're so close to safety."

It was near dawn and they wondered what would await them at their hotel. Luckily, there was no one at the desk when they retrieved their room keys. Afraid to take the elevator, they crept up the stairs.

"We meet in the parking lot in ten minutes, Mark, at my car," Lorraine said. She was shaking from nerves and the exertion of having climbed the stairs.

"Will do," Mark grinned through his grimy face.

Once in her room, Lorraine grabbed a towel and wiped her face, threw off her dirty tee shirt and replaced it with a clean one. She left on her filthy jeans. She grabbed clothing helter skelter and stuffed everything into her beach bag. She retrieved her purse from the wall safe and skittered down the stairs with both bags. It had taken her seven minutes. Even so, Mark was already crouched beside her car. He had stood when Lorraine approached him.

In addition to his knapsack, he held up two bottles of water, like trophies.

Wordlessly, Mark signaled for her to take the wheel. He held his fingers to his lips as a signal for her not to start the motor. She took the emergency brake off and put the gear in neutral while Mark pushed the little French car out of the parking lot and onto the road.

They saw no one.

Once away from the hotel Mark took the wheel and turned on the lights. They both took long gulps of the bottled water, which tasted as good as any vintage champagne, Lorraine thought.

Idling the motor, Mark asked, "Now what?"

"It's late, and if we take the long way back to Dakar, it will be over two hundred miles of land travel," Lorraine said, sighing wearily. She still felt sick to her stomach with nerves.

"Yes, I know. That's the route I took coming here," Mark replied. "It's too long a drive."

"We can't risk waiting at the ferry, the way I came. What'll we do?"

Mark shook his head.

"Let's go to Banjul, in the Gambia," offered Lorraine. "Yes, why hadn't I thought of that before!" she cried. "It's much shorter and we can be first in line in the morning for the ferry across the river there back into Sénégal."

"Here we go!" Mark exclaimed, putting the little Simca in gear. He felt better than he had all night.

The road was paved to Bignona, and they were still very nervous until they were well beyond the cutoff where they had entered the forest with the other crew members earlier.

They made good time, except when they had to slow down to avoid families of monkeys. Theirs was the only car on the road. The Senegalese people avoided driving at night, for many reasons. In the area of Ziguinchor, the local people believed there were spirits about. Then, too, the black mambas lay on the open roads to soak up the heat, and people were afraid in case their cars broke down and they would have to walk.

Only local farmers braved the elements, the nights, the spirits and the black mambas to get their meager goods to market. Lorraine and Mark, too, didn't have the option of worrying about that.

With the dawn came the downpour, turning the road into a mini river. Mark had to slow to a crawl. They drove into Banjul with the gas tank almost on empty. They had even used up the extra gasoline in the jerry can. They bought food and gasoline in Banjul but were still too nervous to eat more than a few bites.

Lorraine's heart was in her mouth when they re-crossed the border back into Sénégal. She thought she would faint when the border guard approached the car. But the guard seemed bored as he waved them through. He didn't even ask for their papers.

They finally felt secure enough to stop at a cafe in Kaolack. Both were exhausted but made another attempt to eat. They took turns using the restroom. Both cleaned themselves as best they could. But Mark didn't shave. He told Lorraine he was afraid of cutting himself, his hands were still shaking from his ordeal.

When her turn came, Lorraine stared at her dull, matted hair and tired, pale face. She hardly recognized the person staring at her from the discolored, cracked mirror. She felt too listless to care.

They resumed their journey, and as they neared Dakar the full import of their deed began to seep in.

Mark spoke for the first time since leaving Kaolack.

"Lorraine, I had better go to the embassy and explain what has happened."

"Why should you, Mark? I'm the producer and director on this project."

"I know, call it old-fashioned chivalry, I guess. I feel I should be the one. Besides, I was responsible for our equipment."

Lorraine still wasn't convinced. "Mark, I think we both should go, but I have no idea how to face Momar and our escort team once they arrive in Dakar," she said, softening.

"Let me do it, Lorraine. You've had a much tougher time than I have." She knew he was referring to her personal relationship with Momar.

She gave in. "All right, Mark," she sighed. "I am grateful. But I need to telephone Micheline. Can we stop at the next pay phone?"

Mark nodded.

A short time later they drew up beside a telephone booth.

Momar didn't waste another minute before sprinting back to where he had left his car. The minivan was still in place, but there was no sign of the film crew.

Momar wondered momentarily if Sam and Diop had been caught by now. He wondered, too, where the ceremonial organizers were holding Lorraine and Mark. But the smoke was getting thicker, and he had to hurry on or he would be overcome.

As it was, he found it difficult to breathe and had a coughing fit once inside his car. He broke speed records returning to Ziguinchor. He refused to think of the ordeal to come.

Back in his hotel room he tried to reason with his turbulent emotions. *How can I ever accuse Lorraine,* ma cherie, *of being part of the conspiracy to film the forbidden ceremonies? She could not have used me because she did not even know I was part of the escort until our meeting in Ziguinchor,* his rational mind tried to reason with him. *But she could be a good actress, the devil in him said. But his reason told him that the shoot had been too well organized to have been hatched only in Ziguinchor.*

He spent the hours before daylight pacing the floor, trying to make sense of the mess. At seven o'clock he telephoned the two other members of the escort team and summoned them to his room.

After briefing them on what he knew, he asked them to return to Dakar and inform the authorities there. He had been further frustrated since he had been unable to reach Dakar by telephone. The telephones rarely worked during *hivernage,* he remembered, and it had been pouring since daybreak.

When the other escorts left, Momar had his chauffeur drive to police headquarters. They had been informed already.

"Still no word about the white man, Diop?" was the first question Momar asked the police chief after the usual long greeting that was necessary before one could get to the point of anything.

"None. Nothing," he replied, hitching up his wrinkled, ill-fitting khaki pants.

"Let us go. Maybe they are with the others," Momar remarked.

"Maybe. Yes," the police chief agreed, coming around to where Momar was standing.

"We take the police jeep," the police chief told him once they were outside in the downpour and he had taken one look at Momar's car. He had no idea that Momar had already taken the car into the forest. Momar didn't argue, just told his chauffeur to wait for him back at the hotel.

The police chauffeur parked the jeep in front of the minivan a short time later. When they arrived at the ceremonial grounds in the glade, there were only two Senegalese men waiting for them. Momar's heart lurched. He was too stunned to speak. Where were the members of the film crew?

The police chief took charge. "Where are the prisoners?"

The voice that had telephoned Momar the night before replied. It belonged to a tall, thin, very black and very angry

Dioula. "The mulatto girl and the white man got away. We lost them." He spat on the ground.

Momar felt sick, weak. "Allah, they are lost in this jungle. Lorraine, *ma cherie.*" He groaned aloud. The other men watched him curiously. Momar wanted to cry out his agony, but he remembered that he was on the circumcision ceremonial grounds and that he had not cried out or sobbed when he was circumcised, and he would not now.

Instead, he asked, quietly, afraid of what his voice would sound like. "What about Diop and the other white man?"

"What? There were others?" the voice asked. Shock showed on both men's faces.

"Let us search the area," the police chief suggested.

They spread out over the charred grounds, which still smelled strongly of smoke. The rain had stopped. They found the hideout with the hunting blind. Momar was the first inside. Sam and Diop's bodies were lying together, unharmed. They could have been asleep, except they weren't breathing.

The others crowded into the blind when Momar called.

A camera on the tripod was still pointed toward the ceremonial grounds. Another one lay between the two men's bodies.

"Smoke got to them," the police chief stated, after examining the bodies.

The two ceremonial officials were stunned. They had been unaware of these two.

"What do we do now?" Momar asked the police chief.

"We have to report them. We can release Diop's body to his family in Ziguinchor. But the American poses another problem." He sighed. *Do I not know it!* Momar felt like adding. "What a horrible mess," was all he could mutter. Where were Lorraine and Mark?

Momar had to control himself. He heard his voice as if it came from far away. "The telephone lines are down," he began, "but I have already sent my two colleagues back to Dakar. They will inform the embassy and the Senegalese authorities."

"We will take the bodies with us, along with their cameras," ordered the police chief. "And we will impound their cameras. Clearly, these are the culprits, but I wonder where the other two are."

They immediately took Sam's body to the shrimp processing plant where they placed it in the freezer to await the arrival of someone from the American Embassy in Dakar.

Because Muslims do not embalm their dead, but bury them as soon as possible, this was the only way to keep the American's body in condition for the trip to Dakar—by refrigerated truck.

Momar knew it was his duty to remain in Ziguinchor to await the person who would accompany it.

He was stuck in Ziguinchor! He thought of Lorraine. A search of the entire jungle area around the ceremonial grounds revealed nothing. Finally, the hotel room held the answer. Lorraine's and Mark's clothes and things were gone, and so was Lorraine's car. After escaping the Diolas, they must have made it back to the hotel and fled.

Was it fear or guilt that made her run away without explanation?

She would certainly return to America and, no doubt, resume her life there. *But she told me that she loves me!* he tried to assure himself. *That was before this mess, you idiot,* his rational mind answered. He knew she could be gone before he got back to Dakar. Maybe she had already left. If only the telephones worked, he thought with a curse. Then he could call Micheline.

After this, what kind of life could I offer her anyway, he thought in despair. Would she even want to live here, after this? He thought of what he had accomplished since his return from the Sorbonne in Paris.

He had become a diplomat with a bright future, until now. His superiors had admired his work; some of his colleagues even envied him. He spoke English fluently, which was a big plus in his profession. *And, yes, just look where it has landed you,* the devil reminded him.

What had he really done for himself?

He had married a woman he did not love. Why? To take the easy way out? Avoid conflict? He was a man now, a diplomat. He should be able to handle this nasty situation. He should be able to handle anything and set it right.

And yet, he reminded himself, he had waited so long before telling Lorraine how he really felt. Maybe too long. Why? Was he afraid? By procrastinating, hadn't he avoided the joy as well as the love Lorraine could have given him? Well, it might be a moot question now, but he had to find out.

He had to get to Dakar before she left, to beg her to tell him her side of the filming fiasco…to ask her to give them a chance. Momar was desperate to tell her that he had faith in her. That he knew she could not have had anything to do with the disastrous situation. The bodies of Sam Benson and Mansour Diop had been discovered with the evidence that cleared her.

Mark Whitman was waiting for Wilson Graves when he returned to his American Embassy office in a nasty mood. Graves had been told to report to the American ambassador and then go to Ziguinchor to pick up the body.

"What the hell happened, Whitman?" Graves bellowed without greeting the tired cameraman. "What's your side of this mess?"

Mark ignored their liaison man's attitude and gave him his abbreviated version of his and Lorraine's ordeal without telling him where Lorraine was. He finished by adding wearily, "I came to inform you and to close up our office here. And wait for Sam to join us."

"Then you haven't heard?" Graves asked, surprised, some of his belligerence gone—although he still glared at Mark as if what he had to say was somehow Mark's fault.

"Heard what?"

"Sam and Diop are dead."

Mark had the impression that Graves delivered the news gleefully.

Mark dropped into the nearest chair. "Do you know what happened?" Obviously he did by the way he was gloating, Mark observed, stunned. Graves told him the Ziguinchor phone lines were finally operational mid-morning. Momar Diallo had immediately telephoned the Foreign Ministry with the entire account.

He scoffed at Mark's offer to accompany him. "It is now a diplomatic affair. Besides, we have the experience," he added. Then he left.

Mark knew he had to inform their New York office so they could notify Sam's family. He also had to pack away their equipment. "What's left of it," he grimaced, remembering the expensive cameras they had abandoned. He knew they would be confiscated as evidence anyway. He wondered if he would have to face charges although he had had no cameras on his person when he and Lorraine had been captured. However, they had been in a restricted area.

"I'll cross that bridge when I come to it," he sighed wearily and began gathering up the things that had to be shipped back to New York.

19

Lorraine leaned back as far as she could in her luxurious seat on the French Concorde and tried not to think. But it didn't work. Her mind reeled off the past forty-eight hours, over and over, like a bad film or a nightmare.

Here she was, on her way to Paris, of all places! That was because the Concorde had been the first airplane out of the Dakar airport on which she could get a reservation. It certainly was the fastest, and she couldn't get away from Sénégal fast enough! She chuckled sadly to herself at that sage observation.

Her mind slid back to the panicked telephone call to Micheline not twenty-four hours earlier. Micheline had answered on the first ring.

"Micheline, it's Lorraine," she had whispered into the pay telephone as the coin dropped noisily. Her eyes had surveyed the area around the telephone booth as if the police would materialize out of thin air.

"Speak up. I can hardly hear you. Where are you? I have been telephoning your hotel every hour on the hour!" her friend had cried.

"Then you have heard what happened in Ziguinchor?" Lorraine asked in a slightly higher, querulous voice.

"Yes, but tell me your side," Micheline said in her always reasonable way.

The American woman gave her Canadian friend a brief report of what had happened in the sacred forest, finishing with, "Mark and I are on the outskirts of Dakar. But with this situation, I dare not return to my hotel. And I certainly can't ever face Momar again, ever!" She had wailed the last phrase.

"Lorraine, listen to me. Come here to my apartment," Micheline replied calmly. "You and Mark both come here and we can work something out."

"Are you sure we won't implicate you by coming to your place?" Lorraine asked, a new worry in her voice.

"So what. You forget I have diplomatic immunity, and who can prove that I know anything about anything?" Micheline countered.

"Well…okay. If you think it's okay," Lorraine had agreed reluctantly.

"Of course it is. I will be on the lookout for your car."

"I have already sent my house servant to send your things here," Micheline was saying. She and Lorraine were seated in her kitchen sipping coffee, Lorraine in a borrowed bathrobe. Mark had just left them, after a badly needed nap, shave, bath and good meal. He assured them that he would take care of everything. Lorraine had showered and washed her hair while Micheline prepared a second afternoon meal for them.

"I don't know how I can thank you, Micheline. I didn't know what to do when we left Ziguinchor. And with

Momar heading our escort! Can you imagine what he must think of me?"

"I have no idea, but he has left a thousand messages at my office and at your hotel," Lorraine's eyes had opened wide as they could.

"I, I can't face him again, ever!" she cried.

"Well, what are you going to do?"

"I'm getting the first flight out, that's what I'm going to do! Unless the police arrest me before I can leave."

"That is running away," Micheline had admonished.

"I know it is, but I can't do anything else."

"You could stay and explain to Momar just as you did to me what actually took place," Micheline had reasoned.

"No! I can't!" Lorraine had wailed.

"What about your work then?"

"I'll write an official report to the ministry when I get home. That's the least I can do," Lorraine answered.

"I cannot change your mind about returning home, then?"

"No. I'm sorry. I have made a terrible mess of everything. You have been an angel, and I really enjoyed the time we spent together." Lorraine hugged her long-time friend, tears streaming.

Later, both had tears flowing when they had embraced at the airport gate. And tears were coming to Lorraine's eyes now, remembering. She closed her eyes and sighed wearily.

"Would *mademoiselle* like champagne?" an elegant French cabin attendant was asking, disturbing her thoughts.

How different from the Air Afrique flight to Dakar, which seemed to Lorraine like a century ago. "Would *mademoiselle* like *champagne?*" Indeed! Why? To celebrate her heartbreak? Her complete foul up on the first important assignment of her career? She felt like turning her back and bawling. But, why not? Why not celebrate the biggest foul up of her life? Why not?

"Oui," she replied to the waiting cabin attendant.

After his first night back in Dakar, Momar awakened at his apartment feeling as if he had a terrible hangover. The brilliant sunshine that had shone while Lorraine and Momar had been at Cap Skirring was gone this morning. There was nothing but emptiness, not just physically but in the knowledge that Lorraine was no longer in Sénégal.

He had to stop thinking about her, he decided, pulling back the sheet and wiggling his toes around on the carpeted floor until he found his babouches. For the time being, he could do nothing about Lorraine's absence. He had to accept it and try as best he could to carry on with his life. The first thing he had to do was to square himself with the ministry. He would feel better the sooner he got that over with.

He was very busy one morning a few days later. There were quite a few official delegations in Dakar, and he was called upon to brief several of them. Momar had not had time today to think of Lorraine, but by mid-morning when there was a break, he began to think about the hundreds of telephone calls he had made to Micheline without success.

At lunch time he impulsively left the Ministry of Foreign Affairs and drove to the Canadian Embassy. Sure enough, Micheline was still at her desk, working away at a huge pile of folders.

Momar thanked the aide who showed him into Micheline's office. She looked up, acknowledging his presence. He could not help noticing that her eyes were red and puffy as she managed a weak smile in greeting.

"*Bonjour,* Micheline," Momar greeted her. His voice was grave.

She returned the greeting in a shaky voice.

"I want to know where she has gone," Momar said, still standing before her desk.

Micheline studied his face for what seemed like minutes, then replied, "She has returned to her office in New York. From there she plans to take a leave of absence at her home town, with her family."

"When did she leave?" he asked, finally easing into the chair beside Micheline's desk.

"Oh, days ago," Micheline said.

"I have not been able to sleep for worrying," Momar said, placing his head in his hands and sighing deeply.

Micheline chuckled sadly, "You think I have been able to?"

"Did you have lunch yet?"

"Are you serious?" Momar asked. "Not only have I not had lunch, I have not had breakfast, Micheline. I have not had a proper meal since I discovered she had left Ziguinchor." He glanced at her. "What about lunch? You look like you lost your best friend." Micheline let out a long sigh.

"Yes, my good friend, whom I had not seen in years, is gone away again."

"Why did you not return my telephone calls?" Momar asked wearily.

"Because before Lorraine called me in Dakar, I knew nothing to tell you; and when she arrived, she insisted that she could not face you," Micheline answered truthfully.

Momar grinned wryly. "I see. Loyalty." Micheline patted his arm.

"Something like that, but she was really in a very bad way, Momar."

Momar did not answer. And later, he did not say much as they munched sandwiches at a restaurant near the embassy. They made small talk until Momar wanted to scream. All he wanted was to have news of how and where he could find Lorraine, and here he was forced to make polite conversation.

But to his surprise, he was hungry. Over lunch, Micheline could see that Momar was really suffering. But what if Lorraine hated her for giving Momar her whereabouts? Finishing her meal, Micheline stood up. She counted out the price of her food plus a tip, and placed the money on the table.

"It has begun to rain," she said, advancing toward the door.

"There is work even when it rains," Momar replied beside her.

Micheline looked up at him. In spite of the lightness of his remark, his face had taken on the same sad look it had when he'd entered her office. There was no way Micheline could not give him the information he needed so badly. She had to help him, she decided, hoping Lorraine would appreciate it in the end.

"Come back to my office. I will give you Lorraine's addresses and telephone numbers," she blurted out.

The look Momar gave her made her heart ache for him. If only she had someone who cared that much about her. But then she did. She suddenly remembered that Mamadou's adoption papers were going through shortly, and soon she would have a son. Someone who loved her and whom she loved. And her relationship with her German diplomat friend was going well, too, she reminded herself further, and smiled.

"You can reach her at her New York apartment if you hurry. Dakar is only six hours ahead of New York time. But she might still be at her office. It is only," she gazed at her wristwatch, calculating the time, "seven in the evening there. She said she had a lot of work to finish before going to her parents' home."

"But I have to go back to the ministry. I cannot telephone America from there," Momar said sadly. "We must use the operator for outgoing calls, and she would never place an unauthorized telephone call."

"You can telephone from my office," she said.

20

"Will that be all, Miss Barbette?" Lorraine's young assistant, Melindy Shaw, asked, reaching for the folder holding the report of Lorraine's work in Sénégal.

Lorraine had telephoned her office from Kennedy Airport and given her boss a quick verbal report of the last week's filming around Ziguinchor. Then she had gone to her apartment, showered, and changed. Now she was leaning forward on her desk, hands clasped together, in a pensive mood.

"Yes, Melindy, and thank you for staying so late to finish typing this stuff."

"That's all right Miss Barbette. Gee, sounds like you had an exciting time," Melindy said, her brown eyes dancing.

"It was, uh…let's say, different," Lorraine said with a sardonic twist to her lips. "I don't think I would want to do it again soon."

"I have asked for a few weeks leave, Melindy. I'm sure you can handle anything that comes up, as you did while I was away."

"Of course. You deserve a rest," the assistant agreed.

"I'll be at my parent's home or at my grandparent's farm. You have the telephone numbers and addresses in case you need to reach me." Nodding good-bye from the open doorway, Melindy closed the door softly behind her. A few minutes later, Lorraine sat in the office of her boss, the company's president and director.

"Really, Lorraine," began Stanton Carter, a middle-aged man whose slight smile softened the angular lines of his face. "You have been through a lot. And your work has earned you a promotion to Executive Producer," he added with a larger smile. "Your films are likely to win a prize."

Before she had left for Sénégal, such a promotion and compliment would have caused her spirits to soar. She would have sent out for champagne for the whole office. But now it was chalk in her mouth. She felt nothing. She thought about Momar and wanted to cry. As a matter of fact, a slight sob did escape her trembling lips. Carter obviously thought it was the promise of the promotion, and she allowed him to think so.

Still smiling, Carter added, "I hope you will enjoy your leave, Lorraine."

"Thank you," she replied, rising and offering her hand in a quick handshake. She met his eyes and saw something that made her feel truly respected as a valuable employee.

"If you like," he suggested, rising to see her to the door, "there is no need for you to return to the office tomorrow before leaving."

"That would be fine," she said, her spirits lifting somewhat for the first time since she had come back to the New York office. The next day found her on another airplane. This time, she was bound for Memphis.

She rented a car, stored her luggage in the trunk, and slowly eased the late model American sedan into the light traffic. How different this large car was from the tiny French-made Simca, she mused, as she turned on the radio and the air-conditioning.

Even with the map on the seat beside her, Lorraine made several false turns before finding Highway 61 South, the route that took her home to Mound Bayou, Mississippi, one hundred miles away.

In an attempt to black out the past few weeks, Lorraine turned up the volume of the radio as high as it would go. There was almost no traffic on the highway and the thought that she was alone was almost her undoing.

An hour and a half later she pulled into the circular driveway of her parents' elegant home. It was gleaming white, two stories high, and fronted by a large flowered terrace. Its porticoed facade was enriched with Doric columns and steps that seemed wider each time she saw them. Two dozen arched windows sparkled in the sunlight.

"Good Lord," her mother cried, uncharacteristically flinging herself from the terrace where she had been tending her beloved roses.

As they came closer together, Lorraine noticed that her mother had not changed a bit since they had last seen each other. Had it only been weeks? She felt that she had aged ten years. She glanced beyond her mother to the lawn, the magnolia tree, the flower beds still riotous with late summer color, the roses.

She held her mother tightly as they hugged.

She found her bedroom just as she had left it, complete with the dotted Swiss canopy and coverlet over the brass bed. Her writing desk, muslin-swathed dressing table, armoire and two chairs completed the decor, along with all of her collection of photographs.

Her private bathroom was just as she had left it, including the bidet she had insisted on having installed during her first vacation home from Montreal. She was glad that the shower was good and hot. She had felt sticky upon arrival.

She had brought one of her Senegalese boubous with her. She decided to wear it this afternoon.

Checking that her makeup and upswept hair were intact, Lorraine took a deep breath and left the room.

Her mother had told her earlier that her grandparents were coming for dinner, and Lorraine knew everyone would be on the terrace. Since the sun was low, it would be cool. She was glad her mother had not invited Andrew. She wasn't ready to face him yet. She knew her family well enough to know they were going to give her the third degree tonight. As she approached them, she heard her mother explaining, "There was some kind of involvement with an African in Sénégal…" Her voice trailed off as three pairs of eyes turned toward the terrace entrance.

Her mother, Vanilla, was elegant in all white. She looked far too young to be Lorraine's mother. Lorraine had inherited her mother's dark hair and her father's gray eyes.

"Grandma! Grandma!" Lorraine literally threw herself at her mother's parents, and they all hugged. Then her grandmother took Lorraine's right hand between both of her own and looked closely at her. "Gal, what you done gone and got yourself into now?"

"Grandma!" Lorraine scolded good naturedly, evading the question. "Let me kiss Papa. He wasn't home when I arrived." Charley Barbette wasn't a big man but had bold, dove gray eyes, a sweep of white-flecked hair and a strong face. Charley held her a full minute, while studying her face thoroughly.

"So you are on a leave of absence,"

"Yes, Papa," Lorraine whispered, taking a seat next to him.

Her mother handed her an iced lemonade as all eyes turned to her again. She knew this wouldn't be easy. Her mother, sensing her unease, came to the rescue.

"Let's go in to dinner," she announced almost immediately, rising. The rest of the family had no alternative but to follow.

But barely after they seated themselves around the table, everyone began questioning her at once.

One by one, her grandmother, grandfather, and father threw questions at her about Sénégal, Momar, and her work there. She didn't tell them about the forest ordeal.

When her grandmother said severely, "But child, how can you expect us to welcome some African who probably doesn't speak English?"

Lorraine was flabbergasted. "Grandma, this isn't like you!"

"But child, we were so worried about you, getting involved with an African, and your colleague dying, and all." Lorraine realized that they were making an African sound as if Momar wore only a spear! She felt like screaming. Instead she asserted, "I'm a grown woman! I've been through a very rough time in Sénégal…"

"We know that, dear, but we only want what's best for you," her mother threw in. Lorraine reminded herself that wanting "what was best" for her included arranging a marriage with Andrew Kemp!

"The African you mention has a name," Lorraine said calmly. "His name is Momar Diallo and he's a highly-placed and respected diplomat," she said proudly.

"Then what would a highly-placed and respected diplomat want with a girl from Mound Bayou, Mississippi?" her grandfather asked, speaking up after a long silence. He obviously hadn't given up the hope that she and Andrew would get back together. Lorraine could practically read his mind.

"We know Andrew," he went on, confirming her suspicions. "We know his parents and his grandparents, my child," he reminded her, peering over his bifocals at her.

They may know Andrew, but, she suddenly realized, they didn't know her at all.

Again she almost screamed. They had been proud of her going to Montreal to university, and again when she had been offered the position with the film company in New York.

But this. This was something they didn't understand.

"He's a diplomat, for heaven's sake! He travels a lot for his country," she said, near tears. She realized it was a lame thing to say, but she also realized why she was fighting so hard for them to accept the idea of Momar. Lorraine knew she still wanted to be part of his life.

"And you would want to live like that?" her mother asked, absently passing Lorraine the steamed vegetables.

Lorraine had no answer.

The next day, as she went about the various domestic tasks, she reflected on what her future should be. When should she return to work? What would she do? Where, if ever, would her next assignment be? And would she ever see Momar again?

The telephone rang constantly—friends and relatives wanting to hear about her African experience. Everyone called—except Momar and Andrew.

21

As the days wore on Lorraine felt a sort of detachment growing over her wounded heart like a scab over a sore. She threw all her energy into helping her mother around the house, but it wasn't enough to distract her from her misery. It was as if misery and pain sharpened her ability when she worked. She was even able to view her promotion with cool detachment.

A few days later she was vigorously polishing the dining room table when she suddenly came to a decision. Hastily scribbling a note to her mother, who had gone off to one of her meetings, Lorraine ran up to her room, threw a few things into a shoulder bag, got her rental car from the garage and headed for her grandparents' farm.

The next morning, a glorious day, she rose at dawn. Donning blue jeans, a plaid cotton shirt and sneakers, she tied a bandana over her hair and headed for the old weather-beaten barn. She had always felt at ease among the farm fowl and animals. Ever since she had been a small child, she had loved feeding them.

After watching the fowl hungrily peck away at the grain she'd given them, she petted the cow and her calf. Then she fed carrots to the horse. Suddenly she felt hungry.

Without waking her grandparents, she prepared her breakfast and ate hurriedly. She made a sandwich and a thermos of iced tea. Those tucked safely away in a lunch pail, Lorraine headed for the red tractor.

"Grandpa mentioned yesterday that he had begun to layaway the cornfield, Brindly," Lorraine told the bleary-eyed old female dog that her grandparents had owned since she'd been a little girl. The old dog seemed satisfied with the girl's explanation and thumped its tail weakly, without rising from the porch.

Lorraine drove the tractor all day, stopping only to refuel from the attached jerry can and stopped only moments when nature called. She had eaten her sandwich and drunk the tea while driving the tractor with one hand.

As she plowed row upon row, turning the tractor expertly at the end of rows, she wondered what Momar, Micheline and the others were doing on the other side of the world. It gave her an eerie feeling to be plowing fields when only weeks previously she had been filming in Sénégal, attending diplomatic receptions, making love with Momar.

"No!" she cried. "I must not think about that! That part of my life is over. Done with!" Yet, no matter how loudly she screamed it, it didn't sound convincing.

When she finally returned to the house, she showered, then put on shorts, a flowered blouse, and sandals. She sat for a quiet moment in the room her grandparents always kept ready for her.

"Lorraine, Vanilla is here, child." Her grandmother's voice floated up the stairs. She hadn't even heard her mother's car arrive.

Lorraine found them seated at the kitchen table, sipping coffee.

"Your father says hello," her mother said conversationally between sips of coffee, adding, "I came to get my regular supply of eggs, milk, vegetables and chickens."

"Would you like some coffee, child?" her grandmother asked, eyeing her closely.

"No, thank you, Grandma, but I would like tea," Lorraine answered, pulling out a chair and sitting wearily. Her grandmother bustled about preparing the tea. Lorraine sighed, realizing how tired she was.

"What are your plans, Lorraine?" her mother asked, watching her daughter as closely as Grandmother had. "Your friends have been asking about you."

"You know this farm belongs to you when we're gone," her grandmother mentioned, setting a delicate tea cup and saucer before her. "And we ain't getting any younger, you know."

Here we go again, Lorraine told herself.

"Your father and I aren't either," her mother added.

Lorraine braced herself for them to add all the old arguments. You owe it to the town founders to marry and settle down here. You owe it to your family. But they were silently watching, waiting for her to answer.

The old-fashioned wall telephone suddenly jangled, cutting the silence.

Her grandmother stared at it as if it were a water moccasin. Still staring at it, she shuffled to the contraption, jerked it off the hook and hollered louder than necessary, "Miller residence."

"Er, would you repeat that, sir?" she asked, holding the telephone away from her ear as if she expected it to bite. "Why, er, yes. Yes, she is. One moment please," she barely whispered.

"It's for you, child," she said.

Lorraine rose stiffly, her eyes question marks, but her grandmother made no comment or explanation as she passed the instrument to her granddaughter.

"Lorraine Barbette here," she said warily into the telephone.

"Momar ici. C'est moi, ma cherie," Momar shouted.

He must think he's still in Sénégal where one has to shout into the telephone to be heard, she thought, as she gasped, almost fainting. She knew he was somewhere in North America because he sounded as if he were in the next room. She leaned against the wall for support.

"Are you there?" Momar asked, still speaking French but having lowered his voice somewhat.

Without thinking, she answered in the same language, her voice suddenly a rasping whisper. With her mother and grandmother now engaged in a rapid low conversation, she asked, "Where are you telephoning from?"

"I am in Montreal, *ma cherie.* Micheline gave me your telephone numbers. I tried to reach you at your office and at your apartment in New York, but you had already left," Momar explained rapidly, then added, "The Foreign

Minister told me that I had to leave right away for Montreal. I am with I.C.A.O."

"I.C.A.O.?" she asked stupidly.

"Yes, it is the International Civil Aviation Organization of the United Nations. You must know it," he replied.

"Ah, yes. I remember now. How did you get this telephone number?" she asked, still stunned, feeling like a clod.

"Your father gave it to me. I have just talked with him," Momar replied. "Before you mention it, I know everything about the Ziguinchor thing, *ma cherie*. It has all been cleared up."

Before she could say a word, Momar spoke rapidly, "We developed the film. We have the goods on your American, Sam, and our Senegalese, Diop," he added.

"Momar, I, I felt so ashamed and humiliated. I felt that there was no way that I could ever face you again. And I also thought you might be implicated, too, and blame me!" she cried. "And, I didn't know how it all would affect your being a diplomat. Oh, Momar, what a mess!"

"It is all cleared up now, *ma cherie*," he soothed. "You and your associate, Mark Whitman, were completely cleared. So do not worry. The ministry did not even blame our team for losing your crew that night because we followed our usual procedure. In fact, we were commended for our quick handling of the matter. So, you see, the whole thing actually helped my career."

"That's, that's good," was all Lorraine could answer, almost collapsing with relief.

"I have a favor to ask though," Momar suddenly announced.

"What kind of favor?" Lorraine asked, warily. Although they had continued to speak in French, she became more aware that she wasn't alone.

"You sound distant," Momar said, sensing her mood change.

"I always sound distant after I have driven a tractor all day, Momar. I am tired," she answered.

"You? You have driven a tractor all day?" He was incredulous. "You amaze me. Whatever were you doing?"

"I was plowing my grandfather's fields." She realized she had never told him that her grandparents had a farm where she had spent most of her childhood.

"I still love you, *ma cherie.*"

"I love you, too, Momar. Still."

"Now say you will do me that favor," he persisted.

"I will do you your favor," she repeated.

"Now say, 'I will join you in Montreal.' "

"I will—What did you say?"

"I want you to come to Montreal. Now. I miss you."

"I miss you, too, but I can't just come to you like that. I have only been here a few days."

Her grandmother and mother were watching her now. Even if they could not understand the language, they seemed to understand the drift the conversation was taking.

"I will pay your airline ticket."

"I can't allow you to do that, Momar."

"Why not? I am the one who wants you to come to me."

"I want to visit with my folks awhile longer."

"Aha! You do not wish to see me."

"Of course I want to see you, but…"

"Then come. I am missing you terribly." He paused momentarily.

"I need you," he added softly.

He certainly knows how to get next to me, Lorraine thought, feeling herself weakening.

Her parents wouldn't be happy to have her go off so soon after she had just arrived. But she'd just have to make them understand.

"Are you thinking it over?" Momar asked after a silent minute, then added, "I hope so."

"I'll pay for my own ticket," she said firmly.

EPILOGUE

Before they returned to Montreal, Lorraine told Momar that she would have to go to New York to square things there.

She had surprised everyone there by resigning from the company. Only Mark knew of her decision and had told her that he would be glad to work with her in Montreal.

Back in Montreal, she had found a small documentary film company for sale. She bought it, and she and Mark set to work. Their first contract was to do a documentary about historical Quebec barns. Lorraine had been so interested in Quebec barns when she was a student that she had done extensive research on them and already knew where most of them were located.

Mark found an apartment and bought new equipment.

The Senegalese government had rented a sumptuous home for Momar in the most elegant part of Outrement, a neighborhood close to downtown Montreal. A home even Lorraine's mother would be proud of, she thought, surveying her domain. She was proud and content.

Momar's arrival from his office interrupted her musings. After soundly kissing her until she was dizzy, he quipped, "Hello, Mrs. Businesswoman," referring to her first dull day at her new company. She quipped right back, after she could control her breathing, "Hello to you, Mister Diplomat."

"I've just arrived, and I love you."

"I love you, too."

Gazing at her longingly, he quoted: " 'Love conquers all.' Virgil."

Lorraine again surveyed her new home and gazed at her husband.

"I'll drink to that, since it's cocktail time."

He followed her to the den and surprised her with a hidden bottle of champagne from the bar's refrigerator.

As she and Momar looked into each other's eyes, she realized that their love had indeed conquered all.

Momar took two frosted champagne flutes from the freezer section of the refrigerator and filled them. He handed her one. "To your success," he said, lifting his glass.

"To us, our countries, and our families. To everyone!" As they clinked glasses, Lorraine realized that she had been right all along to go to Sénégal.

MENUS

...mentioned in Whispers in The Sands

Akara *or* **Accra** *is an entree.*
What you will need for ten people.

> 750 grams of dried beans.
> 1 liter of oil
> 50 grams of pureed tomatoes
> 10 grams of powdered pepper
> 1 onion, chopped

To prepare: Place the beans in a bowl with a bit of water, leaving them until the skins are soaked. Rub them to remove the skins. Leave them for ten hours to soak in clear water. Remove excess water and grind them in a blender.

Add one or two soups spoons of salted water to the ground beans as needed to keep them moist.

Place the oil in a deep fryer. When it's hot, drop small portions of the ground beans into it until they are browned on all sides. When this is finished, if needed, add more oil. Add chopped onion, brown. Add the pureed tomatoes, then the pepper. Add salt, if necessary. Cook for two or three minutes and remove from the stove.

Serve your accra or akara with this very hot sauce.

Bassi salete
For eight to ten people you will need:
> Two kilos of couscous
> 1 large chicken or
> 2 kilos of lamb

1 kilo of white potatoes
500 grams of sweet potatoes
500 grams of manioc (found in West Indian and Chinese
    stores)
1 medium cabbage, cut into four pieces
300 grams of pureed tomatoes
2 or 3 bulbs of garlic
2 laurel leaves
250 grams of dried white
250 grams of dried raisins
half liter of butter
1 liter of cooking oil
250 grams of onions

To prepare:

Peel the vegetables, leaving the potatoes whole, cutting the manioc in medium sized pieces. Cut up the chicken or lamb. Put it with the garlic. Place the oil in a large pot and drop the vegetables, except the cabbage, until they are blanched; add the chicken or lamb. Cook for a few minutes. Remove everything and add the onions until they're opaque. Add the pureed tomatoes. Return the chicken or lamb to the pot. Add salt and pepper to taste. Leave to boil for awhile, add water, if necessary. Add the laurel leaf, the cabbage, cut into four pieces, and the manioc. Cover and cook over medium heat.

Pour the couscous into a large bowl and add a bit of hot water and butter or follow instructions on box. Add the dried beans which have been cooked (or use canned beans), and the dried raisins.

When the cabbage and manioc are almost ready, add all the potatoes. Leave over low heat until everything has cooked. Remove the meat and vegetables to a serving plattter. Stir a bit of the sauce into the couscous.

Serve the couscous and vegetables separately.

Lalo: (I don't think you will find this unless you have Senegalese friends).

Remember when Lorraine and Mark were lost in the jungle and stopped to eat a fruit when she told him that she had seen Senegalese women use the dried, powdered leaves from the baobab tree...? Lalo is what she was refering to.

A *Mechoui* is a whole lamb roasted over an open fire, like an American BBQ.

Merguezes are small spicy sausages made with lamb and spices and served as an entree.

Yassa with chicken

You will need: I chicken 4 lemons juiced, vinegar 3 large onions chopped, salt, pepper, I large hot pepper, chopped

To prepare:

(If you were in Sénégal, you would have begun by plucking and cleaning the chicken!)

Cut the chicken into serving pieces. In a big mixing bowl, add the chicken, salt, black and red pepper, the lemon juice and equal amount of vinegar and two tablespoons of oil, add the onions. Leave to marinate one half hour.

In the meantime, heat up the BBQ. When it's ready, place the chicken pieces on it until they are brown on all sides. Pour the oil into a large casserole, add the onions. After a moment add the rest of the marinade and the grilled chicken. Add a bit of water, cover and allow to cook for ten minutes.

P. S. This dish can also be made with fish or meat. It is served with boiled white rice.

GLOSSARY

Definitions of foreign words used in *Whispers in the Sands*.

Allah, the Muslim God.

Babouches, closed sandals worn in most countries.

Baobab tree, very ancient tree found in Sénégal whose branches resemble arms.

Boubous, floor length square robes worn by both men and women in Sénégal. They can be plain or highly decorated with artistic embroidery.

Benedictine, a sect of Catholic monk.

Bassaris, a tribe in Sénégal.

Ballantes, another tribe in Sénégal.

Balafon, a xylophone type instrument.

Bougeer, two to four drums tied together. The drummer beats them alternately with the palm of his hands.

Djembé, a type of drum used in special ceremonies.

Diola, a tribe in Sénégal.

djellaba, a floor length slim robe, usually trimmed in elaborate embroidery and is worn by both men and women in Sénégal.

Fulani, Momar is a Fulani. A tribe in Sénégal.

Hivernage, the rainy season in Sénégal.

Kora, an instrument not unlike a very large violin except that it is round, has a hole in one side and the strings are vertical gong from the body of the instrument to its tip and is only played by men. Mastering it takes many years and the tradition of playing it is passed from father to son in the section of the tribe called griots. (Griots are the oral historians in Sénégal).

Lebou, a tribe in Sénégal.

Lycée, a secondary school and junior college combined.

Mandingos, a tribe in Sénégal, extending to neighboring countries.

Marfait, a Senegalese dish.

Mechoui, a whole lamb, spiced and herbed and barbecued over an open fire.

Meuzzin, the Muslim priest who calls the faithful to prayers the mosque's minaret or tower.

Ouloff, a tribe in Sénégal.

Piste, a rough road.

Radio Tam Tam, Senegalese for gossipers.

Selbe, the man who sponsors and assists initiates when they are circumcised.

Sérere, a tribe in Sénégal. Ex-resident Leopold Sedar Senghor is a Sérere.

Signarés, light complexioned girls set aside for the white men to use during slavery. They were found only on Goree Island.

Simca, a French-made car.

Tabaski Day, the day Senegalese Muslims celebrate the end of fasting.

Tabla, a long Senegalese drum.

Tanda, a tribe in Sénégal.

Toucouleur, a tribe in Sénégal.

Yassa (see menus)

2008 Reprint Mass Market Titles

January

Cautious Heart
Cheris F. Hodges
ISBN-13: 978-1-58571-301-1
ISBN-10: 1-58571-301-5
$6.99

Suddenly You
Crystal Hubbard
ISBN-13: 978-1-58571-302-8
ISBN-10: 1-58571-302-3
$6.99

February

Passion
T. T. Henderson
ISBN-13: 978-1-58571-303-5
ISBN-10: 1-58571-303-1
$6.99

Whispers in the Sand
LaFlorya Gauthier
ISBN-13: 978-1-58571-304-2
ISBN-10: 1-58571-304-x
$6.99

March

Life Is Never As It Seems
J. J. Michael
ISBN-13: 978-1-58571-305-9
ISBN-10: 1-58571-305-8
$6.99

Beyond the Rapture
Beverly Clark
ISBN-13: 978-1-58571-306-6
ISBN-10: 1-58571-306-6
$6.99

April

A Heart's Awakening
Veronica Parker
ISBN-13: 978-1-58571-307-3
ISBN-10: 1-58571-307-4
$6.99

Breeze
Robin Lynette Hampton
ISBN-13: 978-1-58571-308-0
ISBN-10: 1-58571-308-2
$6.99

May

I'll Be Your Shelter
Giselle Carmichael
ISBN-13: 978-1-58571-309-7
ISBN-10: 1-58571-309-0
$6.99

Careless Whispers
Rochelle Alers
ISBN-13: 978-1-58571-310-3
ISBN-10: 1-58571-310-4
$6.99

June

Sin
Crystal Rhodes
ISBN-13: 978-1-58571-311-0
ISBN-10: 1-58571-311-2
$6.99

Dark Storm Rising
Chinelu Moore
ISBN-13: 978-1-58571-312-7
ISBN-10: 1-58571-312-0
$6.99

2008 Reprint Mass Market Titles (continued)

July

Object of His Desire
A.C. Arthur
ISBN-13: 978-1-58571-313-4
ISBN-10: 1-58571-313-9
$6.99

Angel's Paradise
Janice Angelique
ISBN-13: 978-1-58571-314-1
ISBN-10: 1-58571-314-7
$6.99

August

Unbreak My Heart
Dar Tomlinson
ISBN-13: 978-1-58571-315-8
ISBN-10: 1-58571-315-5
$6.99

All I Ask
Barbara Keaton
ISBN-13: 978-1-58571-316-5
ISBN-10: 1-58571-316-3
$6.99

September

Icie
Pamela Leigh Starr
ISBN-13: 978-1-58571-275-5
ISBN-10: 1-58571-275-2
$6.99

At Last
Lisa Riley
ISBN-13: 978-1-58571-276-2
ISBN-10: 1-58571-276-0
$6.99

October

Everlastin' Love
Gay G. Gunn
ISBN-13: 978-1-58571-277-9
ISBN-10: 1-58571-277-9
$6.99

Three Wishes
Seressia Glass
ISBN-13: 978-1-58571-278-6
ISBN-10: 1-58571-278-7
$6.99

November

Yesterday Is Gone
Beverly Clark
ISBN-13: 978-1-58571-279-3
ISBN-10: 1-58571-279-5
$6.99

Again My Love
Kayla Perrin
ISBN-13: 978-1-58571-280-9
ISBN-10: 1-58571-280-9
$6.99

December

Office Policy
A.C. Arthur
ISBN-13: 978-1-58571-281-6
ISBN-10: 1-58571-281-7
$6.99

Rendezvous With Fate
Jeanne Sumerix
ISBN-13: 978-1-58571-283-3
ISBN-10: 1-58571-283-3
$6.99

2008 New Mass Market Titles

January

Where I Want To Be
Maryam Diaab
ISBN-13: 978-1-58571-268-7
ISBN-10: 1-58571-268-X
$6.99

Never Say Never
Michele Cameron
ISBN-13: 978-1-58571-269-4
ISBN-10: 1-58571-269-8
$6.99

February

Stolen Memories
Michele Sudler
ISBN-13: 978-1-58571-270-0
ISBN-10: 1-58571-270-1
$6.99

Dawn's Harbor
Kymberly Hunt
ISBN-13: 978-1-58571-271-7
ISBN-10: 1-58571-271-X
$6.99

March

Undying Love
Renee Alexis
ISBN-13: 978-1-58571-272-4
ISBN-10: 1-58571-272-8
$6.99

Blame It On Paradise
Crystal Hubbard
ISBN-13: 978-1-58571-273-1
ISBN-10: 1-58571-273-6
$6.99

April

When A Man Loves A Woman
La Connie Taylor-Jones
ISBN-13: 978-1-58571-274-8
ISBN-10: 1-58571-274-4
$6.99

Choices
Tammy Williams
ISBN-13: 978-1-58571-300-4
ISBN-10: 1-58571-300-7
$6.99

May

Dream Runner
Gail McFarland
ISBN-13: 978-1-58571-317-2
ISBN-10: 1-58571-317-1
$6.99

Southern Fried Standards
S.R. Maddox
ISBN-13: 978-1-58571-318-9
ISBN-10: 1-58571-318-X
$6.99

June

Looking for Lily
Africa Fine
ISBN-13: 978-1-58571-319-6
ISBN-10: 1-58571-319-8
$6.99

Bliss, Inc.
Chamein Canton
ISBN-13: 978-1-58571-325-7
ISBN-10: 1-58571-325-2
$6.99

2008 New Mass Market Titles (continued)

July

Love's Secrets
Yolanda McVey
ISBN-13: 978-1-58571-321-9
ISBN-10: 1-58571-321-X
$6.99

Things Forbidden
Maryam Diaab
ISBN-13: 978-1-58571-327-1
ISBN-10: 1-58571-327-9
$6.99

August

Storm
Pamela Leigh Starr
ISBN-13: 978-1-58571-323-3
ISBN-10: 1-58571-323-6
$6.99

Passion's Furies
AlTonya Washington
ISBN-13: 978-1-58571-324-0
ISBN-10: 1-58571-324-4
$6.99

September

Three Doors Down
Michele Sudler
ISBN-13: 978-1-58571-332-5
ISBN-10: 1-58571-332-5
$6.99

Mr Fix-It
Crystal Hubbard
ISBN-13: 978-1-58571-326-4
ISBN-10: 1-58571-326-0
$6.99

October

Moments of Clarity
Michele Cameron
ISBN-13: 978-1-58571-330-1
ISBN-10: 1-58571-330-9
$6.99

Lady Preacher
K.T. Richey
ISBN-13: 978-1-58571-333-2
ISBN-10: 1-58571-333-3
$6.99

November

This Life Isn't Perfect Holla
Sandra Foy
ISBN: 978-1-58571-331-8
ISBN-10: 1-58571-331-7
$6.99

Promises Made
Bernice Layton
ISBN-13: 978-1-58571-334-9
ISBN-10: 1-58571-334-1
$6.99

December

A Voice Behind Thunder
Carrie Elizabeth Greene
ISBN-13: 978-1-58571-329-5
ISBN-10: 1-58571-329-5
$6.99

The More Things Change
Chamein Canton
ISBN-13: 978-1-58571-328-8
ISBN-10: 1-58571-328-7
$6.99

Other Genesis Press, Inc. Titles

A Dangerous Deception	J.M. Jeffries	$8.95
A Dangerous Love	J.M. Jeffries	$8.95
A Dangerous Obsession	J.M. Jeffries	$8.95
A Drummer's Beat to Mend	Kei Swanson	$9.95
A Happy Life	Charlotte Harris	$9.95
A Heart's Awakening	Veronica Parker	$9.95
A Lark on the Wing	Phyliss Hamilton	$9.95
A Love of Her Own	Cheris F. Hodges	$9.95
A Love to Cherish	Beverly Clark	$8.95
A Risk of Rain	Dar Tomlinson	$8.95
A Taste of Temptation	Reneé Alexis	$9.95
A Twist of Fate	Beverly Clark	$8.95
A Will to Love	Angie Daniels	$9.95
Acquisitions	Kimberley White	$8.95
Across	Carol Payne	$12.95
After the Vows	Leslie Esdaile	$10.95
(Summer Anthology)	T.T. Henderson	
	Jacqueline Thomas	
Again My Love	Kayla Perrin	$10.95
Against the Wind	Gwynne Forster	$8.95
All I Ask	Barbara Keaton	$8.95
Always You	Crystal Hubbard	$6.99
Ambrosia	T.T. Henderson	$8.95
An Unfinished Love Affair	Barbara Keaton	$8.95
And Then Came You	Dorothy Elizabeth Love	$8.95
Angel's Paradise	Janice Angelique	$9.95
At Last	Lisa G. Riley	$8.95
Best of Friends	Natalie Dunbar	$8.95
Beyond the Rapture	Beverly Clark	$9.95

Other Genesis Press, Inc. Titles (continued)

Other Genesis Press, Inc. Titles (continued)

Daughter of the Wind	Joan Xian	$8.95
Deadly Sacrifice	Jack Kean	$22.95
Designer Passion	Dar Tomlinson	$8.95
	Diana Richeaux	
Do Over	Celya Bowers	$9.95
Dreamtective	Liz Swados	$5.95
Ebony Angel	Deatri King-Bey	$9.95
Ebony Butterfly II	Delilah Dawson	$14.95
Echoes of Yesterday	Beverly Clark	$9.95
Eden's Garden	Elizabeth Rose	$8.95
Eve's Prescription	Edwina Martin Arnold	$8.95
Everlastin' Love	Gay G. Gunn	$8.95
Everlasting Moments	Dorothy Elizabeth Love	$8.95
Everything and More	Sinclair Lebeau	$8.95
Everything but Love	Natalie Dunbar	$8.95
Falling	Natalie Dunbar	$9.95
Fate	Pamela Leigh Starr	$8.95
Finding Isabella	A.J. Garrotto	$8.95
Forbidden Quest	Dar Tomlinson	$10.95
Forever Love	Wanda Y. Thomas	$8.95
From the Ashes	Kathleen Suzanne	$8.95
	Jeanne Sumerix	
Gentle Yearning	Rochelle Alers	$10.95
Glory of Love	Sinclair LeBeau	$10.95
Go Gentle into that Good Night	Malcom Boyd	$12.95
Goldengroove	Mary Beth Craft	$16.95
Groove, Bang, and Jive	Steve Cannon	$8.99
Hand in Glove	Andrea Jackson	$9.95

Other Genesis Press, Inc. Titles (continued)

Hard to Love	Kimberley White	$9.95
Hart & Soul	Angie Daniels	$8.95
Heart of the Phoenix	A.C. Arthur	$9.95
Heartbeat	Stephanie Bedwell-Grime	$8.95
Hearts Remember	M. Loui Quezada	$8.95
Hidden Memories	Robin Allen	$10.95
Higher Ground	Leah Latimer	$19.95
Hitler, the War, and the Pope	Ronald Rychiak	$26.95
How to Write a Romance	Kathryn Falk	$18.95
I Married a Reclining Chair	Lisa M. Fuhs	$8.95
I'll Be Your Shelter	Giselle Carmichael	$8.95
I'll Paint a Sun	A.J. Garrotto	$9.95
Icie	Pamela Leigh Starr	$8.95
Illusions	Pamela Leigh Starr	$8.95
Indigo After Dark Vol. I	Nia Dixon/Angelique	$10.95
Indigo After Dark Vol. II	Dolores Bundy/ Cole Riley	$10.95
Indigo After Dark Vol. III	Montana Blue/ Coco Morena	$10.95
Indigo After Dark Vol. IV	Cassandra Colt/	$14.95
Indigo After Dark Vol. V	Delilah Dawson	$14.95
Indiscretions	Donna Hill	$8.95
Intentional Mistakes	Michele Sudler	$9.95
Interlude	Donna Hill	$8.95
Intimate Intentions	Angie Daniels	$8.95
It's Not Over Yet	J.J. Michael	$9.95
Jolie's Surrender	Edwina Martin-Arnold	$8.95
Kiss or Keep	Debra Phillips	$8.95
Lace	Giselle Carmichael	$9.95

Other Genesis Press, Inc. Titles (continued)

Last Train to Memphis	Elsa Cook	$12.95
Lasting Valor	Ken Olsen	$24.95
Let Us Prey	Hunter Lundy	$25.95
Lies Too Long	Pamela Ridley	$13.95
Life Is Never As It Seems	J.J. Michael	$12.95
Lighter Shade of Brown	Vicki Andrews	$8.95
Love Always	Mildred E. Riley	$10.95
Love Doesn't Come Easy	Charlyne Dickerson	$8.95
Love Unveiled	Gloria Greene	$10.95
Love's Deception	Charlene Berry	$10.95
Love's Destiny	M. Loui Quezada	$8.95
Mae's Promise	Melody Walcott	$8.95
Magnolia Sunset	Giselle Carmichael	$8.95
Many Shades of Gray	Dyanne Davis	$6.99
Matters of Life and Death	Lesego Malepe, Ph.D.	$15.95
Meant to Be	Jeanne Sumerix	$8.95
Midnight Clear	Leslie Esdaile	$10.95
(Anthology)	Gwynne Forster	
	Carmen Green	
	Monica Jackson	
Midnight Magic	Gwynne Forster	$8.95
Midnight Peril	Vicki Andrews	$10.95
Misconceptions	Pamela Leigh Starr	$9.95
Montgomery's Children	Richard Perry	$14.95
My Buffalo Soldier	Barbara B. K. Reeves	$8.95
Naked Soul	Gwynne Forster	$8.95
Next to Last Chance	Louisa Dixon	$24.95
No Apologies	Seressia Glass	$8.95
No Commitment Required	Seressia Glass	$8.95

Other Genesis Press, Inc. Titles (continued)

No Regrets	Mildred E. Riley	$8.95
Not His Type	Chamein Canton	$6.99
Nowhere to Run	Gay G. Gunn	$10.95
O Bed! O Breakfast!	Rob Kuehnle	$14.95
Object of His Desire	A. C. Arthur	$8.95
Office Policy	A. C. Arthur	$9.95
Once in a Blue Moon	Dorianne Cole	$9.95
One Day at a Time	Bella McFarland	$8.95
One in A Million	Barbara Keaton	$6.99
One of These Days	Michele Sudler	$9.95
Outside Chance	Louisa Dixon	$24.95
Passion	T.T. Henderson	$10.95
Passion's Blood	Cherif Fortin	$22.95
Passion's Journey	Wanda Y. Thomas	$8.95
Past Promises	Jahmel West	$8.95
Path of Fire	T.T. Henderson	$8.95
Path of Thorns	Annetta P. Lee	$9.95
Peace Be Still	Colette Haywood	$12.95
Picture Perfect	Reon Carter	$8.95
Playing for Keeps	Stephanie Salinas	$8.95
Pride & Joi	Gay G. Gunn	$15.95
Pride & Joi	Gay G. Gunn	$8.95
Promises to Keep	Alicia Wiggins	$8.95
Quiet Storm	Donna Hill	$10.95
Reckless Surrender	Rochelle Alers	$6.95
Red Polka Dot in a World of Plaid	Varian Johnson	$12.95
Reluctant Captive	Joyce Jackson	$8.95
Rendezvous with Fate	Jeanne Sumerix	$8.95

Other Genesis Press, Inc. Titles (continued)

Revelations	Cheris F. Hodges	$8.95
Rivers of the Soul	Leslie Esdaile	$8.95
Rocky Mountain Romance	Kathleen Suzanne	$8.95
Rooms of the Heart	Donna Hill	$8.95
Rough on Rats and Tough on Cats	Chris Parker	$12.95
Secret Library Vol. 1	Nina Sheridan	$18.95
Secret Library Vol. 2	Cassandra Colt	$8.95
Secret Thunder	Annetta P. Lee	$9.95
Shades of Brown	Denise Becker	$8.95
Shades of Desire	Monica White	$8.95
Shadows in the Moonlight	Jeanne Sumerix	$8.95
Sin	Crystal Rhodes	$8.95
Small Whispers	Annetta P. Lee	$6.99
So Amazing	Sinclair LeBeau	$8.95
Somebody's Someone	Sinclair LeBeau	$8.95
Someone to Love	Alicia Wiggins	$8.95
Song in the Park	Martin Brant	$15.95
Soul Eyes	Wayne L. Wilson	$12.95
Soul to Soul	Donna Hill	$8.95
Southern Comfort	J.M. Jeffries	$8.95
Still the Storm	Sharon Robinson	$8.95
Still Waters Run Deep	Leslie Esdaile	$8.95
Stolen Kisses	Dominiqua Douglas	$9.95
Stories to Excite You	Anna Forrest/Divine	$14.95
Subtle Secrets	Wanda Y. Thomas	$8.95
Suddenly You	Crystal Hubbard	$9.95
Sweet Repercussions	Kimberley White	$9.95
Sweet Sensations	Gwendolyn Bolton	$9.95

Other Genesis Press, Inc. Titles (continued)

Sweet Tomorrows	Kimberly White	$8.95
Taken by You	Dorothy Elizabeth Love	$9.95
Tattooed Tears	T. T. Henderson	$8.95
The Color Line	Lizzette Grayson Carter	$9.95
The Color of Trouble	Dyanne Davis	$8.95
The Disappearance of Allison Jones	Kayla Perrin	$5.95
The Fires Within	Beverly Clark	$9.95
The Foursome	Celya Bowers	$6.99
The Honey Dipper's Legacy	Pannell-Allen	$14.95
The Joker's Love Tune	Sidney Rickman	$15.95
The Little Pretender	Barbara Cartland	$10.95
The Love We Had	Natalie Dunbar	$8.95
The Man Who Could Fly	Bob & Milana Beamon	$18.95
The Missing Link	Charlyne Dickerson	$8.95
The Mission	Pamela Leigh Starr	$6.99
The Perfect Frame	Beverly Clark	$9.95
The Price of Love	Sinclair LeBeau	$8.95
The Smoking Life	Ilene Barth	$29.95
The Words of the Pitcher	Kei Swanson	$8.95
Three Wishes	Seressia Glass	$8.95
Ties That Bind	Kathleen Suzanne	$8.95
Tiger Woods	Libby Hughes	$5.95
Time is of the Essence	Angie Daniels	$9.95
Timeless Devotion	Bella McFarland	$9.95
Tomorrow's Promise	Leslie Esdaile	$8.95
Truly Inseparable	Wanda Y. Thomas	$8.95
Two Sides to Every Story	Dyanne Davis	$9.95
Unbreak My Heart	Dar Tomlinson	$8.95

Other Genesis Press, Inc. Titles (continued)

Uncommon Prayer	Kenneth Swanson	$9.95
Unconditional Love	Alicia Wiggins	$8.95
Unconditional	A.C. Arthur	$9.95
Until Death Do Us Part	Susan Paul	$8.95
Vows of Passion	Bella McFarland	$9.95
Wedding Gown	Dyanne Davis	$8.95
What's Under Benjamin's Bed	Sandra Schaffer	$8.95
When Dreams Float	Dorothy Elizabeth Love	$8.95
When I'm With You	LaConnie Taylor-Jones	$6.99
Whispers in the Night	Dorothy Elizabeth Love	$8.95
Whispers in the Sand	LaFlorya Gauthier	$10.95
Who's That Lady?	Andrea Jackson	$9.95
Wild Ravens	Altonya Washington	$9.95
Yesterday Is Gone	Beverly Clark	$10.95
Yesterday's Dreams, Tomorrow's Promises	Reon Laudat	$8.95
Your Precious Love	Sinclair LeBeau	$8.95

Order Form

Mail to: Genesis Press, Inc.
P.O. Box 101
Columbus, MS 39703

Name _____
Address _____
City/State _____ Zip _____
Telephone _____

Ship to (if different from above)
Name _____
Address _____
City/State _____ Zip _____
Telephone _____

Credit Card Information
Credit Card # _____ ☐ Visa   ☐ Mastercard
Expiration Date (mm/yy) _____ ☐ AmEx   ☐ Discover

Qty.	Author	Title	Price	Total

Use this order form, or call 1-888-INDIGO-1	Total for books _____
	Shipping and handling: $5 first two books, $1 each additional book _____
	Total S & H _____
	Total amount enclosed _____

Mississippi residents add 7% sales tax